RAISING EACH OTHER

A Book for Teens and Parents

Jeanne Brondino, Shellie Brann,
Scott Coatsworth, Heidi Sonzena,
Cheryl Swain and Fran Tulao

alias The Parent/Teen Book Group

Hunter House

Hunter House Inc., Publishers
P.O. Box 847
Claremont, CA 91711-0847

Library of Congress Cataloging-in-Publication data

Raising each other.

1. Adolescence. 2. Parenting—United States. 3. Youth—
United States—Attitudes. 4. Parents—United States—
Attitudes. I. Brondino, Jeanne. II. Parent/Teen Book Group
(Etiwanda High School)

HQ796.R34   1988   305.2'35   87-21354

ISBN 0-89793-044-4

Cover design by Qalagraphia and the Parent/Teen Book Group
Cover art by Teri Robertson
Editing by Chris Moose and Kiran S. Rana
Production by Paul Frindt
Set in 10/13 Palacio and 10/12½ Nashville by Highpoint Type
and Graphics, Pomona, CA.

Manufactured in the United States of America

9 8 7 6 5 4 3   First edition

CONTENTS

FOREWORD
by Jack Canfield
vii

INTRODUCTION
How It
All Started
1

CHAPTER 1
Teens' Biggest
Problems
6

CHAPTER 2
Parents' Biggest
Problems
26

CHAPTER 3
If I Were
A Parent
57

CHAPTER 4
Rules To Live By
That Are Fair To Everyone
83

CHAPTER 5
Three Things
I Would Change
114

AFTERWORD
141

ABOUT THE AUTHORS
142

LIST OF
CONTRIBUTORS
148

Dedication & Acknowledgments

The Parent/Teen Book Group would like to dedicate
this book to Hunter House Publishers. They deserve
recognition for believing in this project and working
with us all to make *Raising Each Other* a reality. We
especially want to thank Luis Caughman and Paul Frindt
for sharing their skills and time so freely with us;
Chris Moose, Judy Hamilton and Gurubanda Khalsa for
their advice, encouragement, and support; and Kiran Rana,
without whom none of this would have been possible.

FOREWORD

How many books have been written about teenagers and their relationships with their parents? Probably hundreds, most of them by professionals in counseling or education. What makes this book special is that it is a report from the trenches—and what a delightful report it is! Written by five high school students and their English teacher, *Raising Each Other* is alive with the actual words and feelings of teens and parents today.

As a worker in the field of self-esteem, with many years of experience with students, this book impresses me. The efforts of the authors have paid off. *Raising Each Other* will give comfort to any teenager or parent who believes he or she is alone with unsolvable problems, and will provide insight about teenagers and their personal opinions for any educator, counselor, or other interested professional.

The story of how this book was written illustrates the effectiveness of self-esteem in the high school setting. The students who wrote the essays used in the book gained from being listened to seriously. Once they felt that their own feelings and opinions were validated, they were able to be open to their parents' views, and a deeper and more honest level of understanding was possible. Another lesson to be taken from this book is that, if given an opportunity and some guidelines, teenagers are capable of thinking deeply about teen problems and ways to resolve them.

Another important contribution of *Raising Each Other* is that it shows the accomplishments students are capable of. Adults who make disparaging remarks about teenage laziness and lack of commitment should look at this work by the five students of the Parent/Teen Book Group and revise their opinions. The Parent/Teen Book Group spent over a year organizing, writing, editing and illustrating this book. They typed the manuscript into a computer, appeared in radio and TV interviews, and wrote to local and national magazines and newspapers. They showed by their sustained effort and their wonderful product that students can create something that they and the rest of humanity will find meaningful and worthwhile. Students *can* make a real difference.

The book shows deep thought about the hazards of the teenage years and it also expresses a deep compassion for the dilemmas of parents. The chapter on "Rules To Live By That Are Fair To Everyone" shows that parents and teenagers have ideas that are more similar than either would have ever imagined. Another chapter, "If I Were A Parent," goes straight to the heart with its plea for honesty, love, compassion, and trust in the parent-teen relationship.

Raising Each Other is a testimonial to American teenagers' capacity to think, work, and strive for a deeper understanding of themselves and their parents. It deserves to be read, both for its accomplishment and for the important message it contains.

Jack Canfield
Pacific Palisades, 1988

HOW IT ALL STARTED

This book is different from every other book about teen-parent relationships. For one thing, it is almost entirely written by teens. We feel it accurately reflects the views of teens today, while giving real attention to the problems parents face. Secondly, the way it came about was unique. We decided to tell the story behind the making of this book so that the reader will know who "we" are and understand why the book was written.

Raising Each Other grew out of five essays and the class discussions of two eleventh grade English classes at Etiwanda High School in California. The essays were written by about fifty-five students, and each topic developed from the previous one. The teacher had not planned a series of essays; what started as an attempt to get her students to write well about something—anything—snowballed into an unusual and wonderful classroom interaction.

The first paper was an extra credit assignment. The teacher had just graded essays that the students had written about American Indians and the results were discouraging. It was clear they were not really involved with the subject. Abandoning her lesson plans, the teacher looked for something closer to home, something the students could relate to. Her choice: Write an essay on "Teens' Three Biggest Problems."

The results were electrifying. The students knew their subject, of course, but what came as an eye-opener was their eagerness to express themselves. Most students said parents were their biggest problem, with school a close second. After lively classroom discussions, the teacher decided that the students needed another assignment—another point of view. She told them to interview two parents of teens and then write a paper about *parents'* biggest problems. Again, the response was amazing. Many students, showing a real desire to understand their parents, reported their problems and opinions in depth. These two assignments became the basis for Chapters 1 and 2 of this book.

A surprising thing began to happen. Students who usually never participated, who had never been willing to open their mouths about native American culture or the economy, came to class eager to talk about teen and parent problems. Discussions were heated; there was a lot of laughter. Everyone was alert. Obviously, something was working.

One of the comments that came up repeatedly was, "I wouldn't do that IF I WERE A PARENT," which almost always led to the question, "Well, WHAT WOULD you do?" which almost always brought the answer, "Well, I wouldn't do it THAT WAY." It was time for another assignment, and the teacher asked, "HOW WOULD you do it?" Chapter 3 contains the response: how these teens said they would raise their own teenagers "If I Were A Parent."

In every discussion the students were very concerned about what was fair to teens. The teacher was also concerned about what was fair for parents. This led to the fourth assignment: Create "Ten Rules to Live By That Are Fair to Everyone." The results appear in Chapter 4. Chapter 5, the concluding chapter, is more personal. It grew out of a paper the students wrote on "Three Things I Would Change." Although it is not specifically about parent-teen relationships, this chapter reveals a great deal about the lives and feelings of teenagers and parents, and should be of interest to both.

The idea of turning these class papers into a book occurred simultaneously to two students, who later became members of the Parent/Teen Book Group, and to a publisher-friend of the teacher who was looking for books on teenagers. The students, half-kidding, told the teacher one day, "We should write a book about this." The publisher, inspired by the story of the classroom interactions, suggested, "We could make a book out of this—and teach interested students about publishing at the same time." So the teacher asked the class: Are any of you interested in working on a book based on what we have been doing?

She had her doubts. Teenagers, she thought, just aren't that interested in books. They won't be patient enough to make the long haul from rough manuscript to bound volume, to draw illustrations, write ad copy, and learn all the other details of making and marketing a book.

She was wrong. Twenty students were interested. Meetings began, first at the school, then at the publisher's office. Pretty soon the group consolidated into a core dozen or so who could commit their time and energy to the project. Three months later, five students, the teacher, and the publisher were left, self-dubbed "The Parent/Teen Book Group." There were now decisions to be made—and much to learn.

Our group called itself the Parent/Teen Book Group and began to meet whenever time allowed. At first we tried to analyze the papers, but we soon gave up. This was how the "experts" did it, but we were no experts. Instead, we decided that each paper should be allowed to express itself, give its own point of view. And so our book became a book of many voices, and we let it say what it actually said, not what we wanted to hear. We as a group contributed the graphics; we added transitions to bridge the gaps between different topics; we gave organization to the different chapters and we added a scenario at the beginning of each one to relate that chapter to real life. But beyond this, the book remains a collective voice, asking for understanding on both sides.

Parent input for the book came at two different times. The information for "Parents' Biggest Problems" was gathered by the teens through interviews with parents. Thirty-six students who completed the assignment interviewed two parents each; hence, this chapter draws upon the opinions and experiences of seventy-two adults. After they had decided to write this book, the Parent/Teen Book Group asked a number of parents to complete shorter versions of the assignments used for Chapters 4 and 5: "List Ten Rules to Live By That Are Fair to Everyone" and "What Are Three Things You Would Change." Seventeen responded, and their answers are included as a representative sample of adult attitudes about these topics.

The Parent/Teen Book Group read the essays and scratched their heads over how they would present them. They selected typical, or unusual, or insightful extracts from the different essays; these they pushed and pulled into a rough draft of a manuscript. They drew many illustrations and selected about sixty of them to place in the text. They wrote scenarios: typical situations that would remind the reader of everyday family reality. They input the manuscript on computer, wrote news releases, and spoke on radio stations. By the time they graduated from high school they thought they were done. They had spent a year of Saturdays working with their teacher and the publisher. They were tired.

Why all this work? After all, they had been warned by the publisher that their chances of becoming rich and famous were small. They had already decided to donate one-third of their royalties to their high school library. Elsewhere in this book the members of the group describe themselves and discuss their individual motivation. As a group, however, they had a very definite goal:

> The purpose of our book is to foster understanding between teens and parents, and to show each side how the other feels. It also tells teens and parents that they are not alone; that there are others who are facing the same problems and trials.

In writing the chapters, the Parent/Teen Book Group used the class papers like an opinion poll, counting the number of times issues were mentioned or griped about. Of course, no sociologist would accept these classes as a "significant" sample of the teen population, and this book does not claim to present any statistical norms, but here is a profile of the students: They all attended Etiwanda High School, in the western end of San Bernardino County in Southern California. This is a comparatively new high school in a fast-growing suburban area about one hour east of Los Angeles. The students were mainly middle-class teens from upwardly mobile families. Many of them had or wanted jobs and cars; when teenagers reach sixteen or seventeen, getting a car, and the freedom that provides, is very important. As their own writings show, emotionally and intellectually they seem to be a normal, average group of sixteen- and seventeen-year-old American teenagers.

A note about the editing: The Parent/Teen Book Group corrected the spelling in the papers. Grammatical errors, however, were usually left alone. Quotations were not chosen for their literary style but for their content—as representative samples of what students and parents have to say about some important topics.

We believe we have succeeded. And we believe that the statements presented here will be read with recognition and a sense of revelation by both teens and parents.

Each of us has been through his or her own trials as we have written this book. They have drawn us together, five teens and one teacher with very different lifestyles and ideas. We still have some conflicts within our families, and our values have not drastically changed, but we as friends have drawn upon one another's strengths to try again. And, as we keep trying, we understand that there can be no such thing as a perfect family. The best we can do is learn to understand—and raise each other.

Sincerely,

Cheryl Swain
Heidi Sonzena
Fran Tulao
Shellie Brann
Scott Coatsworth
Jeanne Brondino

alias The Parent/Teen Book Group

1

TEENS' BIGGEST PROBLEMS

LAST CHANCE
FOR THOSE OF YOU WHO DIDN'T DO
THE ASSIGNMENT ON THE AMERICAN INDIANS:

WHAT ARE TEENS' 3 BIGGEST PROBLEMS?
1. _____
2. _____
3. _____

WRITE A 500 WORD ESSAY ON THESE
FOR EXTRA CREDIT —
                    DUE MONDAY!

RENEE: A SCENARIO

It was a school night and Renee was sitting in her room. She felt as if she would explode, because she knew what would happen to her later in the evening. Her hands were cold and clammy and her stomach was in knots. She was only seventeen years old and already failing in this world.

Her heart jumped to her throat as she heard the front door open, then slam shut. Dad was home and she was in for it. Her mother had called him at work to tell him what had happened—he had not been very pleased with what he had heard. Now Renee heard his bellowing voice as he called for her to come out of her room...

At one time or another in our lives, most of us have felt the way Renee does. That terrible feeling that everything is going all wrong and no one understands is one we've all experienced. Life's problems, tough at any age, seem more than just tough during adolescence. But that's what being a teenager is all about.

This chapter is based on twenty-two essays written by high school students about their three biggest problems. In reading and re-reading the papers, the Parent/Teen Book Group found that the problems mentioned most often were parents and school. Next came "friends," a category covering a wide range of concerns about teens' relationships with their peers. Most papers discussed these three things in one way or another, and the following essay is typical.

>>> PARENTS, SCHOOL, FRIENDS...

Today's teenagers' biggest problems have to do with their parents, work in school, and their friends.

Teenagers have many problems but one of the biggest problems they have is with their parents. Nowadays teenagers like to get what they want, and if they don't, they would get mad and start to throw things around. Some parents just don't let teenagers have any fun. They won't let you go out until they have met the guy you're going out with. Parents just don't trust us teenagers any more. And when teenagers can't take it any more they run away. I have a friend who had a boyfriend who is black. Her parents are totally against black people and when they found out about her boyfriend, they kicked her out.

The second biggest teenage problem is about school. They can't keep up with the work because of their boyfriends or other friends. It causes a big problem. Some teachers just give a lot of homework and they don't understand that students have other homework in other classes. It takes a lot of time from us teenagers even though it is good for us. But then we should think about the quote, "Business before pleasure."

The other biggest problem for teenagers is their friends, which turn into enemies sometimes. A lot of friends depend on other friends too much. I sometimes feel like my friends are just using me for things, but when I have a problem they help me. I've known a friend for about six or seven years and she just started to flip out. Once she met a guy and started to go out with him, she would have me take her to his house in my car. I've tried to talk to her but she just won't talk to me. I considered her as a best friend a long time ago, but now I don't talk to her any more. It hurt me for a while but I still have other friends.

All of these problems are capable of being solved. Some teenagers are too confused to solve their own problems. That's what counselors and Dear Abbeys are for. I should know about these problems because I'm a teenager myself and I've had to solve these problems without any help.

As this paper shows, all three areas—parents, school, and friends—are interrelated. Parents have an effect on their teenagers' relationships with friends; friends have an effect on teens' schoolwork, and so on. But it is also clear from the essays that if these three areas concern teens the most, the real "hot spot" when it comes to talking about their problems is their parents.

PARENTS: AUTHORITY, RULES, REBELLION...

How do teens see their parents? Who *are* parents to teenagers—how do they become these Jekyll-and-Hyde figures who change at a moment's notice from "Mom" and Dad" to interfering strangers? Maybe the answer is that during adolescence the way teenagers view themselves changes radically, and so does their view of everyone around them.

Below, teens talk about their parents and the problems they face with them. Some of the struggles will sound familiar, such as the age-old conflict between the "oppressive" authority figure and the "rebellious" adolescent. Very often the conflict starts over authority but then quickly boils over to include everything else.

>>> Many rules parents set down can become a problem. Curfew is one of the worst. If a child disagrees with his curfew he or she will argue, which only causes major problems. Parents love to "put down" their kids' friends. To them every girl is a slut and every boy is a sex maniac. Of course school is at the top of the list. If you haven't done ten hours of homework, it is not enough. Probably the teenager's worst fight with their parents is about developing a habit. One habit in particular is smoking. Many teenagers are smoking. Many teenagers start smoking out of peer pressure, but those people don't usually end up making it a habit. The opinions of teenager smoking differ from parent to parent. Most parents will not let their child smoke because they feel they're not old enough yet. This only causes the child to add more smoke to the lungs, because kids love to do what parents don't want them to do.

It is natural that rebellion should be focused on parents, because they are the closest authority figures around.

>>> Rebellion is a way to get back at people who set our ground rules and regulations. "Be home at ten!" and get home at eleven. "Do your homework!" "My dog ate it!" Most teenagers want nothing more than independance and to feel free, and to feel old! Most of us often state that we're old enough to take care of ourselves and we don't need our parents! A lot of people will do anything just to not do what they're told. But sometimes it really can be serious when parents won't let go and refuse to give their kid a chance at enjoying life in any way. Then there are the kids who cling to their parents, who want desperately for their kid to be more active in life. In any circumstances, though, the answer for the

vast majority of the teenagers is rebellion, which is simply expected and accepted as a fact of life from a lot of adults nowadays. Not a good fact, but a fact.

Of course, rebellion is rooted in the desire for independence that, in many ways, is the whole business of being a teenager. The teens who wrote the following were certainly identifying major sources of rebellion.

>>> Parents are very hard to please. Most parents guide and direct their teen too long. During adolescence, the teen wants to feel and be self-reliant. This situation causes conflicts between the parents and the teen. While the teen tries to become independent the parents tighten their hold of the teen. This problem could be solved by the parent trying to stay in the background and letting the adolescent try his or her own independent way.

>>> Some people say teenagers are too young to go out on dates. They always keep an eye on teenagers and never leave them alone. There is always something a teenager can't do.

>>> Another place of authority conflict may be from the law. Drugs make up a big part of this problem. Friends put pressure on a person to take drugs or alcohol, which are both against the law. Since parents and police are ALWAYS telling teenagers not to smoke pot or take drugs, much of the natural urge to rebel arises and many teenagers wind up in trouble as a result.

One idea suggested by the above excerpt is that parents are often inclined to look for solutions that lay down the law; for the line that is tough, straightforward, and simple. Maybe it's time to give some thought to this. At one time or another *everyone* rebels, not just teens, and the idea that harsh rules promote rebellion is not new. So, are parent rules sometimes making matters worse?

THE OTHER SIDE: RESPONSIBILITY, UNDERSTANDING, ADJUSTMENT

Many teens realize that their problems with parents are two-sided, and that teens can earn their parents' trust and a greater degree of freedom by showing responsibility.

>>> Many teens argue with their parents. Teens always want to go to a party, or movies, or out cruisin' with a bunch of friends, and their parents won't allow them to. Then the teen gets all upset and wants to run away or something. Teens must get their parents' trust first before they are allowed to go out. They should also earn the privilege to go out, by doing housework or something. They can't expect to just sit around the house doing nothing and get to go out on weekends.

>>> Parents are problems sometimes and are helpful most of the time. They won't let us do something and we get mad at them. Most of the time it's for our own good. They are protective of things we do. When we get in trouble or something we get mad at them. But most of the time they are right. For example, I got in trouble because I was bike racing with a broken arm. I used to BMX race. I was grounded until I got my cast off.

One teen saw the whole parent-teen relationship as a "period of adjustment," when teens are learning to be on their own but cannot be given total freedom.

>>> When teenagers reach adolescence, they are approaching a period of adjustment in their lives, a period of beginning to make their own decisions, being able to recognize right from wrong, and learning to take responsibility for their own actions. In doing this, teenagers begin to move a little further from their parents. They might feel they know what's best for themselves, and their parents should no longer make rules or decisions for them. It's a difficult period for them because

they are no longer children, but they also cannot be allowed to do whatever they wish. This sometimes results in arguments between teenagers and their parents. Sometimes misunderstanding occurs. Maybe the teen feels his parents are saying "no" just because they don't want to let the teen have fun, when really they feel it would be to his benefit if they said "no" once in a while. Parents can see the negative aspects of situations better than the teen can at times, and sometimes this can cause conflict.

There are some deep insights about both teen and parent problems here, not just complaints. What's more, many of these statements do more than list the problems—they offer solutions, some philosophy, and a bit of humor. Teens are looking ahead, too. As one teen put it,

>>> The all-American teen problem with parents is "They just don't understand." They expect more when you give your best. They start getting really picky about your curfew and dating. They think the whole world is out to kill or destroy their child. But as the teens grow up, the parents ease off, and life goes on.

SCHOOL: A TEEN'S NUMBER ONE JOB

School tied with parents as the major complaint of the teens who wrote these essays. Gripes about school ranged from too much homework and unfriendly teachers to pressure over grades and parents insisting on their children doing well in school before they could have the freedom to have a job or an active social life. "From my own personal experiences," wrote one teen,

>>> school has been my number-one problem in life. In order to get certain opportunities from my parents, I have to be doing well in school, first. The pressure from parents and teachers is so strong, I don't see how anyone could do bad in school on purpose.

Another teen wrote her entire essay on the conflicts between school and work.

>>> GETTING BOTH DONE

A big problem teenagers have is keeping up with their homework and going to work to earn money.

To some, getting money right now is just as important as homework, and to some, they say "Who cares about homework? I want some CASH!" So that's exactly what they do; they work all the time and never can find time for their homework. All they're thinking of is their car expenses, clothes, etc. They're not thinking though what Mom and Dad will do if they don't have good grades. For most, it's no more car and no more socializing.

But to get both done is quite an accomplishment. You figure you go to work right after school and don't get home 'til 10:00. Then after you're home, you pull out the books and do the studying. You've completed a hard day. Then you go to bed and before you know it, it's 7:00 A.M. and time to start a new day. When do you get a break? NEVER! You just gotta hang in there and tell yourself you can make it. It's a tough job but someone's gotta drive to school and have a car to go out with on the weekends. You just look at it as though you're pretty special. It's what keeps you going, knowing you have got something now and you'll have something in the future with your schooling.

It is important to remember that these students are sixteen or seventeen years old and are very interested in getting a car and driving. Their big urge is to "get wheels" so they can get around and increase their freedom. In many ways their struggle to keep up with school and earn some money and have fun is a very adult balancing act, and the pressure over school can lead to "burnout" for even the very motivated student.

>>> Trying to get through school is a tough problem. The teachers seem to give too much homework, the classes seem too hard, and the only thing likable in school is lunch-time. Most teenagers get tired of school by their senior year in high school. This causes many problems with future education. The teen is so burnt out with school that he doesn't even want to go to college.

For the teen who falls behind, a downward spiral can be the result. Many teens begin to ditch classes and end up failing or dropping out.

>>> School is one of the main problems teenagers have. Homework is very hard to keep up, and seems to pile up rapidly when one has five to six classes. This causes many kids to feel restricted and feel an urge to ditch school for some free time. When one feels held down he tends not to do well, and grades often turn out very badly. Some feel that grades are a big problem.

>>> Many people have homework almost every night and they may find it difficult to keep up. Some teens don't seem to care at all about their grades, which usually means they fail, and have to make it up again anyway.

These comments suggest that school is a serious source of pressure for teens. To some, it is an obstacle between them and what they really want (a job, a car, special privileges). To others it is an unavoidable necessity: "It's what keeps you going, knowing . . . you'll have something in the future with your schooling." Is there *any* way to make school more enjoyable?

FRIENDS

School does provide the major meeting ground for teens and their friends, and in at least one paper, school got an "A", not for academics but for atmosphere:

>>> The classroom is a friendly atmosphere where we are surrounded by many people we know. It is hard for teenagers not to associate with people sitting around them.

The interaction teenagers have with their friends is often the best part of their lives. They depend on their friends for social activities, fun, and gossip. A teen's friends can usually understand his or her problems and offer advice. Friends, most teenagers will agree, are extremely important. Yet the teens who wrote these essays also mentioned friends as a large problem in many of their lives.

>>> We also have problems with friends. For example, say we have a best friend and we get mad at each other, then we get in a fight. We have to be careful to pick good friends who have the same interests and other things in common. Most of my friends I know are from sports.

>>> Friends are a wonderful thing to have, but problems often occur. They get in arguments over simple things. One person doesn't talk to another and an argument begins. Boyfriends and girlfriends can also irritate one another. They don't have enough time for both each other and their friends.

>>> Another common problem with teenagers is fighting with their friends. The fight may be because of a competition of seeing who is the most popular between friends. Another reason could be because two guys fight over a girl. Friends will always try to compete.

As the last two comments make clear, relationships with the opposite sex are a big concern. Apart from the question of sex, many teens feel pressured to have a boyfriend or a girlfriend as a measure of their social status.

>>> Boyfriends and girlfriends are another form of peer pressure. If a boy or a girl doesn't always have a person of the opposite sex next to them, they feel like trash. "I'm fat and ugly and I hate myself as much as everyone else does." That is the kind of comment from a very insecure teenager who needs someone constantly there to be happy.

Teens also feel a great deal of pressure to "fit in" with a certain crowd. And there are lots of different groups, defined by their dress, haircut, slang, and musical preferences.

>>> One of biggest problems teens have is being accepted by all of their friends in school. They have to dress right, talk right, listen to the "in" music, and be "totally cool." If a teen doesn't do all these things, then he is either weird or "totally out of it."

>>> The problem concerning teenagers and their peers is that they have to live up to certain standards or they'll be considered a goon. You must do and have many things in common with your friends or they won't be your friends.... Many teenagers get into certain groups, and often these groups get into many conflicts with each other.

>>> School is the main source of peer-pressure. It doesn't make any sense. Everyone wants to be themselves yet they all put up a front. I don't need the front, and neither do they. Everyone else tries to be "cool." They pressure each other into doing things they don't want to do. It's true, I've done plenty of things I haven't wanted to do.

>>> Some teenagers are pushed into peer pressure by their parents. Parents sometimes don't realize that teenagers need a little more attention than their younger brothers and sisters because they are nearing adulthood. Instead of giving them attention, parents give them responsibility. More responsibility than they can handle. When they feel that the responsibility is too much they resort to doing things that they see other kids their age do, like smoking, drinking, stealing, and sometimes drugs.

PEER PRESSURE, DRUGS, SEX

When peer pressure becomes so great that it goes beyond dress, speech, and music—when it becomes so great the teen finds himself doing things he doesn't really want to be doing—it goes beyond "cool." Four of the twenty-two essays listed drugs as one of the three major problems teens face; five essays mentioned drugs in relation to peer pressure.

>>> They all suck each other in, telling each other how "good" it is, when often times they haven't even done it themselves. They say, "Oh, come on, it's only one line, coke can't hurt you." That's what makes up tomorrow's drug addicts. It really makes no sense why we tear each other like that.

>>> Drugs nowadays are practically the biggest problem kids go through. Getting high at school in restrooms is very popular, and leaving the campus to smoke it. There are so many people in our community alone who use drugs that everyone is influenced to do the same.

>>> This has got to be the number one problem of today's teenagers. It's not just drugs alone, but also alcohol and marijuana. It seems many teens are pushed into it by peer pressure. Others seem to turn to it as a way out of

other problems, but they're really turning into a bigger problem.

Although these papers are being used anonymously here, they were written in an English class as essays to be graded. Some students probably did not write about drugs, even though they may have considered them to be one of teens' three biggest problems. On the other hand, certain students may have written about drugs for the shock value. In either case, the link between drugs and friends shows the stress teens experience from peer pressure.

Sex was seldom mentioned in the papers; most teens were more concerned with drugs. Again, this is probably not a good indication of the extent to which the teens were sexually active, and the connection between sex and peer pressure was clear just the same. One girl whose entire paper focused on peer pressure stated the problem plainly.

>>> If he asks you to have sex with him and you say NO he often leaves you for another girl. So you begin to wonder if he would still be with you if you had had sex with him. So if the situation occurs again you do it. This often results in teenage pregnancy. A very big problem among teenage girls. Their parents sometimes neglect them because they are disappointed, their boyfriend leaves them and they are left with a baby, no father and no parents for guidance.

The two quotes below are from boys:

>>> Every time a boy sees a girl, the first thing that pops into his head is sex, and not whether she's a nice girl or not. When guys are sitting in classrooms girls distract the boys so then it's harder to concentrate.

>>> Girlfriends keep you from school too. You're so wrapped up in her that's all you think about all day. When you think, you daydream, and when you daydream you miss out in class. Then all your friends get mad at you for spending all your time with her. Then if you're not careful accidents can happen. You're in trouble unless you have the money on hand. But some girls want to keep their babies. Then it's your responsibility too to help take care of it. Then you wind up getting married and there goes a lot of your plans for the future. Some people get married at eighteen. So if the husband wanted to go to college he wouldn't be able to because he would have no way to support his family. In other words he would have to get a job. All I could say is to not get too close.

One girl writer indicated how devastating it is when sex fails to keep a relationship going:

>>> A teenage girl, usually in fear of losing someone she loves, often turns towards the sexual relationship. And if

this does not work out she will feel very lonely, empty, and confused. This will lead her probably straight to an attempt of suicide. A teenage guy, on the other hand, usually turns to the use of drugs . . . until he can't handle it and then he may turn to a suicide attempt too.

ADOLESCENCE: A FAST BOAT IN ROUGH WATERS

The last excerpt may be overstated: The Parent/Teen Book Group found only two references to suicide in all the papers. Nevertheless, issues such as suicide and some others which were not mentioned at all—homosexuality, AIDS, child abuse and other violence in the home—are touchy subjects, difficult to discuss under the best of circumstances and certainly unlikely to be mentioned in an English paper that is going to be graded. It is hard to tell how much of a problem exists in these areas: probably more than meets the eye, perhaps less than fearful parents imagine. As one writer put it, many things a lot less sensational than sex, drugs and rock 'n' roll are a lot more real and important to adolescents:

>>> Their emotions start becoming very touchy, and they don't understand why. They also start getting acne, which they feel will never go away. I know acne doesn't seem like such a big deal, but to most teens it's their biggest problem they've ever had.

Quite a few students mentioned adolescence as a problem in and of itself. They seemed to understand that the change from childhood to adulthood is rocky, and they took a philosophical attitude toward the process.

>>> The reason why teenagers have so many problems is that we have uneven social, mental, physical, and emotional growth. If the teens talk to their parents, teachers,

or friends about their problems, they will probably be able to handle their problems much better.

>>> I feel that teenagers have a lot of problems. It is just part of life to have problems. When we grow up to adult stage we won't have as many problems but we always will have problems. I think a person who had no problems would be boring because they would never change moods or their style. People learn from their problems.

>>> Although teenagers face a lot of problems, they sometimes learn to deal with them. After all, this is still the most exciting time of our lives.

2

PARENTS' BIGGEST PROBLEMS

ASSIGNMENT:
INTERVIEW 2 PARENTS & WRITE A
SHORT ESSAY ON <u>PARENTS'</u> 3 BIGGEST
PROBLEMS —
1. _____
2. _____
3. _____

DUE FRIDAY

WORKING MOM: A SCENARIO

Work that day was hard. A thousand memos covered her desk, waiting to be typed. The phone rang incessantly. She had been late for work, and she was tired from the previous evening out. At lunch someone had spilled hot coffee on her, and now she was miserable.

The clock's hands seemed fixed in place, ticking and ticking but getting nowhere. Every time she looked up it was the same. Finally, blessedly, it was five o'clock.

She waited in the parking lot for her daughter to pick her up. After a while she gave up and got a ride from a co-worker.

As they drove up to her house, she let out an involuntary gasp. There was the car, the entire rear end crushed, sitting in front of the house. Absolutely furious, tired, and miserable, she rushed into the house, demanding to know what had happened. Her daughter sat there in her latest punk outfit, staring back disrespectfully. Then the girl got up and, with an angry look at her mother, ran to her room and slammed the door. Her mother followed her down the hall and, through the closed door, demanded an explanation.

As seen in the scenario above, outside factors frequently aggravate the relationship between parents and teens. Whether we are teens or adults, we all occupy more than one world. There are the worlds of job, family, and school, to name a few, and the people and problems of one world frequently impinge on the other worlds which demand our attention. In the previous chapter we saw how teens juggle the grueling cycle of school, work, and home. In this chapter parents talk about about some of the pressures they face, and how these affect the parent-teen relationship.

The chapter is based on papers written by thirty-six students. (How these teenagers ended up writing about parents' biggest problems was explained in the Introduction, but is repeated here briefly.) In their papers on teens' biggest problems the students had complained bitterly about their parents. Their teacher, a parent of two teenagers herself, felt that parents were getting unfair press, so her second assignment to her students was as follows: Interview two people who have teenage children. They may be your parents, or they may be anyone else you know who has teenagers. Each interview should last about fifteen minutes. Ask your subjects to discuss their three biggest problems. Do not lead them in any direction, do not prompt them with questions such as "Well, what about your teenagers?" Just let them talk, even if they do not mention their teens at all. Take notes during the interviews, and from your notes write a paper about parents' biggest problems.

PARENTS' PROBLEMS: THE BIG THREE

To identify the most common problems of these adults, the Parent/Teen Book Group categorized the responses reported by the students. This was not easy. Many problems overlapped, such as job worries and financial problems. Stress—especially the wear and tear that results from worrying about past, current, and future problems—was a major problem in itself, not easily identified with a single aspect of life yet connected with everything we do and hope to do.

Eventually, the group came up with the following categories, ranked in order of importance:

1. Money	mentioned in 34 papers	
2. Teenagers	" " 30 "	
3. Job	" " 17 "	
4. Marital problems	" " 13 "	
5. The future	mentioned indirectly	
6. Social concerns	mentioned once or twice	

In comparing parents' problems with the most common concerns of the teens, the group noted two interesting differences. First, adults seemed to experience more stress as a result of *fears or worries* over what *could* go wrong in their lives. Second, they were more likely to voice a concern for the welfare of others—their children or society at large—than were the teens. Not necessarily because they are less self-centered than teens but because they are more likely to see how the welfare of their spouses, their children, and society in general directly affects their *personal* welfare, and their concern with these areas is an extension of their self-concern.

The paper that follows is quite typical in content: the biggest problems mentioned are teenagers, job dissatisfaction, and money. The parent's tone, however, which is highly critical of teenagers, is not so typical. The majority of papers, as we will see, were more thoughtful and self-questioning.

>>> TEENAGERS, FINANCES, AND JOBS

I interviewed two parents who both happened to agree pretty much on the same things. They both agreed that teenagers, finances, and jobs were pretty much at the top of their list for parents' problems today.

The first adult I interviewed seemed to think that we as teenagers should take on more responsibilities and we should have more respect and join in more with family discussions instead of staying secluded away in our rooms. She also doesn't like us coming home and then cleaning up and leaving again. This adult also commented that all we want is things for ourselves and we don't care about anyone else. She also said that we are very expensive and that all we do is ask for things and that we never take any time to give in return.

One of the other problems this adult has is with job dissatisfaction. She says she works too hard and doesn't make the money she should, and she doesn't even know why she stays because she doesn't like the job. She says her boss is an ignorant jerk and he is always yelling at someone and he is constantly making people upset. She says he is a very crude person and she wishes she were able to quit.

The second adult that I interviewed also said teenagers were one of her biggest problems. She says we don't listen and we are constantly running up the phone bills and we are always messing up around the house. She says that we should be with the family more often too, and she also said we should consider our parents' feelings about things more often instead of only thinking of ourselves.

Another problem that this adult has is money. She says her bills are ridiculous and her job doesn't pay enough for all the food, utilities, and home costs that she needs. She said that she wishes she had a better paying job, shorter hours, and she wants to be able to come home, sit down and just relax instead of having to worry about other things.

In conclusion I think these two adults seem to agree pretty much. Their top three problems were teenagers, finances, and jobs. I think that parents and teenagers both need to work harder on their problems; maybe then some of their problems can be worked out.

"WHAT'S THE MATTER WITH TEENAGERS TODAY?"

Although "Money," appearing in thirty-four of thirty-six essays, headed the parents' problems list, we decided to discuss parents' problems with teenagers first in this chapter. This seems justified: Concerns about teens ran a close second to money, and in many of the papers the references to money appeared in connection with the expense of raising teens. And at least one student reported that the parents she interviewed considered their teens' problems to be their problems too.

>>> The problem that both [of the parents I interviewed] seemed to agree upon was about their children. The explanation I received was how most of the teenagers' problems somehow became the adults' problems also. Another was trying to get the child to follow a "straight and narrow path in life" without any serious problems

with school, drugs, or members of the opposite sex. Driving is another important issue that a number of adults see as a big problem with their teenagers. For fear of an accident starts the process of worry.

These parents were obviously concerned about many aspects of their teenagers' lives, a response that was typical of many parents. When the papers in which teens were a major parental concern were analyzed further, the biggest concerns about teens were, in order:

1. Parent-teen communication
2. Expense of raising teens
3. Drugs
4. Education
5. Moral values
6. Driving
7. Teens' ambition
8. Discipline
9. Teens' friends
10. Sex
11. Peer pressure
12. Mistakes
13. Respect for others

Obviously, a list like this is both revealing and misleading. For one thing, it says nothing about the *degree* of concern expressed by different parents. For another, the list is almost equally divided between "known" problems or fears, and unknown problems. Known problems include issues like communication and discipline which parents deal with every day; unknown problems include uneasiness about whether teens are sexually active or drive too fast. The expense of raising teens was a major specific or known problem, while drugs, the third-ranked concern, was more often mentioned out of the parents' anxiety about their children rather than because of actual evidence of drug use. One writer noted that his subject felt "indirectly threatened" by drugs because he worried that his teenager may be influenced by **peer pressure** to experiment with them. Most parents have similar fears.

> > > One of the things they worry about is their kids not getting molested, or anything like that. They may also worry about their teenagers being into drugs or not. Many adults would like their kids to grow up in a respectable manner and with a good education.

> > > They are worried about their children being pressured into drugs and alcohol. They also worry about their children doing well in school. Another problem is their teenagers getting their license. When teens take the car out parents hope that they will be mature enough to drive safely and not show off and kill themselves. Parents also want to make sure that they taught their children well enough so that when they leave home they will be able to make it on their own.

> > > I think adults that have teenagers are worried about their teenagers experimenting with drugs. Parents are aware of the drug problems and what drugs can do. They do not want their children to end up dead because they overdosed. Parents are afraid for their children and hope that they would have enough common sense to say no.

Sex was mentioned less often, although the direct teen-parent interview format may have inhibited some parents. However, one parent seemed to understand it well:

> > > Sex is also a very real pressure on teenagers at a young age. It's hard to explain to teenagers, when they're feeling very adult anyway, that there really is a right and a wrong time for sex. Hopefully, we've kept the lines of communication open enough so that they'll talk to us about sex and birth control before engaging in either.

Parents commented on their concern with the **general moral values** held by their teens.

>>> One lady said her goal was to try and keep her kids on a straight path and expressed the worry involved with her children's moral decisions. All the time and effort of setting a good example for her kids is beginning to pay off, but the worry will always be there.

>>> [The parents I interviewed] feared that their child was in this stage where he would resent punishment. They didn't know how to deal with the teenager when he did something wrong. They felt that their child had different religious and moral values. What was wrong to parents once now seemed okay to teens. Even though they had all of these problems with their teenage children, they still loved them very much.

This mention of the age-old generation gap brings us to the concern most often expressed by the parents: **communication** with their teens. This issue seems to take precedence over all other concerns in the attempt many conscientious parents make

to understand what their teens are going through. As one parent put it, "Hopefully, we've kept the lines of communication open enough...." The operative word here is "hopefully": whether they express it or not, parents have many hopes, fears, and doubts about their relationship with their children, and a deep need to share their feelings and know what is happening.

>>> One of the big types of problems seemed to be for them to be able to communicate with their teens. Their opinions were different from the teens' in almost every way. The parents had a hard time being able to understand the teens' opinions in music, school, and the way they live their life. Worrying that something bad might happen to them or them doing things wrong. The parents seemed very concerned about the lack of communication with their teens.

>>> Another problem that seemed to plague them was communicating with teenagers. They found it hard to talk with their teenaged kids because they (the kids) had become strangers that resented having rules forced on them. As parents, my subjects found it difficult to deal with this rebellion in any other way except to add more

restricting rules. My first subject said that adults were afraid to be honest with their children, because it showed that they weren't perfect. My second subject thought there wasn't enough communication because both parties were unwilling to give in to the other, make the first move.

>>> Parents don't know about the things that are going on in their children's lives, and, the way I see it, children know even less about their parents. Before I really started talking to my mother (one of the people I interviewed), I didn't know that we had so many things in common, and that we have similar feelings about many things. She told me that she'd never known about all the things that were going on in my mind. Now that we know more about each other, it's easier for us to talk to one another.

Like the writer of the last excerpt, several of the students, as a result of the interviewing process, saw adults' concerns from a new angle—and the perspective was not always a pleasant one!

>>> My biggest problems [one parent said] are my four children. They are so demanding and thoughtless, also very irresponsible. I don't have a moment that I can call my own. I work four days a week. On my days off I run the children to school, doctors, dentists, dancing lessons, gymnastics, and attend their football games. The only thing that they can tell me is that I nag them. What keeps me going is that they are good children and I love them all very much. I suppose this is what being a mother is all about.

>>> One of the parents thought that children were adults' biggest problems. When I asked what age group he thought caused the most problems, he replied "All." He commented on how children don't listen to their parents. It doesn't matter what age the child is, they never

seem to listen to what parents have to say. He thinks that once children reach a certain age they start to believe that their parents don't know anything. This causes conflict between the two, which makes the life at home miserable.

The children of the interviewee were actually present during the following interchange:

>>> The first person I interviewed was my friend's mother. She said that her kids are lazy, they never want to do anything around the house, and they are uncooperative. Her kids were all sitting around listening to the interview and denying everything. It was quite funny. She also said her children resent being told what to do, and think she is totally unreasonable.

The next set of parents sound really angry. In fact, this quotation is included over the protests of more than one member of the Parent/Teen Book Group, who were extremely angered themselves over what this parent had to say about teens' **morals.**

>>> The home life with the kids was the major problem with the two people I talked to. They stated that their children don't do what they are told and that they never listen. When they are asked to do something such as clean the kitchen, they give their parents a hard time about it and ask "Why?" One person I talked to even went so far as to say that he believed many of today's teenagers have no moral values and that they don't care about the future of the country.

Many parents expressed their worries, not as anger at their teens, but as a deep anxiety over their own parenting abilities and performance. They seemed to have done a great deal of thinking about being fair to their children and treating them equally. They were concerned about **setting a good example** for their children and hoped they were preparing their children adequately for future independence.

>>> When I asked the father alone what he felt were his biggest problems he replied, "I find that teaching my children to stay out of trouble and keep up in school is one of the largest problems I have." He said that he wished he had time to express how important it was for his children to stay away from drugs, from alcohol, and to set good and strong goals in life. He's afraid that, considering the fact that he's hardly home to do the disciplining, they might have to learn about life the hard way.

>>> When I talked with one lady, she said that she feels a certain amount of insecurity with parenting, because she doesn't know if they [she and her husband] are doing the right things for their children and giving their children the right things. She said that since there is no

way to go to school to be a parent, like for example an electrician, "you just have to learn from your parents and hope they prepared you correctly."

That last line made us stop and think a long time. And the young parent who is quoted below also seemed to suggest that the lack of "preparation" can be a trap when it comes time to try open communication:

>>> As a young parent, trying to communicate with my teenagers on a one-to-one basis is one of my big problems. Being a young parent, in my early thirties, trying to communicate with my teenagers over situations that have or may occur during their teenage years. Remembering back less than twenty years ago, I don't feel there's much of a generation gap but being a parent of teenagers, I find it very hard to relate without taking a parental stand. Only because my teenagers think there

is a generation gap, I find their needs and their wants harder to meet. Probably because I have still not met all my goals that I know I could have met earlier for myself and my family, friends, and other people that tried to help. Trying to relate these facts to my teenage kids, I see them listening to me as much as I did at their age, to my parents, that were trying to help me. Therefore, I get frustrated, upset, and take my parental stand, which I thought at eighteen years old I would never do to my family because of the way it was done to me. As a young parent of teenagers, I find it hard and sometimes embarrassing disciplining them for their mistakes when I'm still making mistakes myself, which can involve them or their lifestyles with me.

Parents show a complex array of responses to the problems teenagers present them. The papers expressed frustration, anger, depression, insecurity, and confusion, but also thoughtfulness, questioning, and hope. Most of the parents interviewed appeared to be doing their best to "keep the lines of communication open." At the same time, they realized that, even when they are convinced that their own lessons and examples are sound, they can't be sure the teen is listening:

>>> It's unsettling when you can't be sure if all the good things you try to teach your teenagers can so easily be shoved aside when they are around their peers.

Perhaps one reason that the parents interviewed were such great worriers has to do with this loss of control. Then again, being a parent of a teenager, in many ways, *means* letting go.

MONEY—IT MAKES THE WORLD GO 'ROUND

Money was parents' number one concern. In fact, only two papers did not mention money at all. Some parents discussed it directly, complaining about bills and debts, and many mentioned it indirectly, referring to the extra expenses of raising teenagers.

>>> Both people I interviewed were concerned with their many debts. Everyday expenses and the cost of raising a family on a tight budget is leaving them little extra. The general worry of how and when they were going to pay these bills was apparent throughout the interview. One expressed the importance of not getting into debt in the first place and always saving a little extra. Money is probably the most common problem of adults, married or single.

>>> I read in the papers that the economy was getting better; well my two subjects didn't agree. I was told that while they are making more money, it doesn't seem to go as far as it used to. Bills are getting higher and higher for less service. The cost of keeping a car running and buying gas for the car amounts to quite a lot. Both of my subjects agree that teenagers use up money faster than anything else. All of this doesn't leave much for recreational spending, not to mention buying what they want.

Many parents related money problems to worry about **inflation, Social Security,** and **retirement.**

>>> They don't have enough money to live the way they want to. They have teenagers and are spending a lot of money on them. Adults are often worried about the future. What should they do with their money? When they are ready to retire they want to have money in the bank to live on. Social Security is an important thing to older adults who are retired. Adults have many problems with money and have to solve those problems before they get too old.

>>> Inflation is rising very fast and it is hard to live on a fixed income. Social Security won't cut it; sometimes retired adults have to take a part-time job to pay for food, clothing, and housing. I think that adults hate to see the day when they have to retire because they are afraid of finances.

Some feared a future depression.

>>> They were afraid that they wouldn't be able to get by in the world with the changes in Social Security laws and rules, inflation, and the economy today. Some of the adults were afraid that eventually we would once again drop into a depression. Adults feel that the dollar is losing its value and that they won't be able to live comfortably in today's world.

One set of parents wanted to make sure that their children would not worry about money, and so hid financial troubles from them.

>>> The family was another problem. Making sure they had enough money to buy food and pay bills. Doing these duties took a lot of effort and care because if something was wrong they didn't want their children to think that they didn't have enough money and didn't want their children to start worrying; they want their family to feel secure and live happily.

The biggest problem seemed to be that parents just didn't have enough money. This came through especially clearly when the subjects were divorced.

>>> Since both women are single they have to help to support the family and with three kids it's kind of hard especially since kids always need or want something. They also have to worry about paying all kinds of bills. They also need to have money for emergencies and un-

expected things that come up. They also feel bad when they can't give their kids things that they would like to.

> > > Second to be interviewed was my mom's boyfriend. His biggest problem is financial. He has two teens; one is sixteen years old and the other eighteen, and out of high school. He's living with his parents, until he can find an affordable house or apartment to live in. He doesn't have much money to spend on my mom, mainly because he just bought himself a new car and had to buy his daughter a used car for her own transportation. His eighteen-year-old son can't find a job and he borrows money from his dad to fix his car and take out his girlfriend. His [my mom's boyfriend's] biggest problem is a financial problem.

Even in the one paper, given below, in which the parents interviewed were obviously financially secure, money was a preoccupation. The paper is also unusual because the parents' desire for money is not just to make ends meet but to be wealthy. And it is unusual for yet another reason: The parents did not even mention their teens.

> > > BASICALLY GOAL-ORIENTED
The problems of adults seem to vary but I seemed to have encountered some problems in my interviews such as trying to make enough money and trying to attain educational and financial goals. Both people I interviewed did not seem to mention their teenage children at all. They seemed to be wrapped up in other things, basically goal-oriented.

The first problem I encountered was coming from the woman I interviewed. She basically said that she was worried about holding down her business, run with two other people, and trying to attain her Ph.D. at the same time, which can be quite a stressful situation. She needs to work toward her goal but at the same time make sure she takes care of her other responsibilities. She reported planning her daughter's wedding as the only other problem.

The second person I interviewed could only tell me about one big problem. He said that he was worried about making enough money so that he can live very luxuriously. He wants to be able to have a house in Switzerland, a house in England, and a house in America. He works all the time and tries to find ways to make extra money too. So he is still trying to reach his goal.

As I can see the two individuals I interviewed, both are trying to attain the goals they have not achieved yet. In general I think more and more people are striving to attain their goals and they do not have a lot of time to worry over their teenage children.

The paper above seems "out of sync" with the other comments about money. Perhaps having enough money does reduce the day-to-day concerns so evident in the other parents' worries; on the other hand, the people could also be too busy to notice problems that are closer to home.

JOBS

Jobs were mentioned in fifty percent of the papers as a major source of concern for parents. Since jobs determine people's financial stability, this section is closely connected with concern over money. Worries about jobs also connect with concerns about health, retirement, and future **financial security.**

>>> One lady was worried about her husband's health at work and his possible early retirement. This would cause even more financial troubles. The alternative would be to risk his health, in which case the outcome could be far worse. The second lady was concerned with a possible layoff at her job.

>>> One parent said that he was more concerned about keeping his job once he got older. When people are younger they don't really need to keep a job. There's usually other jobs that they can find. When people grow older and have a family, keeping the job that they have becomes a bigger concern, because their families are at stake. They need the job to support that family.

>>> The job status was another concern, trying to keep a job and being happy with it. One of the women was concerned with her husband's physical condition in the line of work that he is doing. Retirement is another concern related to job status. As a person gets older and plans for a retirement, it requires deep thought, careful planning, and worries a lot of people.

Day-to-day existence at work can also be very stressful, and that was the theme in several papers.

>>> She also has problems getting along with people at work, in particular management. Her boss, she says, is discriminatory against women and carries a "chip on his shoulder" all the time. He just brings a bad attitude to work every day. Another problem she has at work is having a time limit or a deadline for everything. This puts a lot of stress on her by the end of the day, and when she comes home it is usually in a bad mood.

>>> There are problems that both the father and the mother have. They both feel that there's an enormous lack of communication between them and their teenagers or children. They feel that their jobs take up too much of their time, and because their teenagers are getting older they're not around as long. So there just aren't enough hours in the day to talk to each other, and to do things together.

>>> One of the most common problems was lack of recreation. With the adults I interviewed I found that they felt

ousy or they don't have the

or spend some restful time at

:. I was also told that this feel-

scape work put a lot of stress

:s even to the point of causing

1, another of their problems.

aced as boredom with work, a

en.

bored with their jobs easily,

nging jobs constantly. This is

:d, but for the not-so-well-

educated it's very hard. A lot of people are just not am-
bitious enough to get up and find something new. So
they just sit around unhappily waiting for someone to
offer them a new job, which rarely happens.

>>> Many adults are only qualified for jobs consisting of
menial tasks. Now that they're older, they're bored with
their jobs, and they have no way of transferring to another because they have had no training in any other
field.

>>> Another problem that both women talked about is jobs.
One said that she needs a job that pays enough to help
support her family and that will be worthwhile and interesting. The other woman also feels that what her
friend said is important. At her work she isn't kept busy
enough so she gets bored. This is very frustrating for her
because she said it's hard to work somewhere that you
don't feel needed.

The job of **housewife** had its drawbacks too—financial and
otherwise.

>>> The mother has many problems that have to do with her
job as a housewife. She feels that she does too many
monotonous tasks. Because of these little chores, she

can't do the many things that she wants to do. This makes another problem for her, not enough time to spend with her husband.

>>> Another problem she had was the running of the house. She had to clean up messes, wash clothes and dishes. She had to make sure everything was done. She also had to make sure that all the bills were paid. She didn't work [at a paying job]. She was a housewife whose husband works and she worried about getting enough money to pay the bills.

Like the woman in the scenario that opens this chapter, working parents bear the double burden of meeting others' expectations of them both on the job and with the family. Still, one parent, who holds two jobs, was able to laugh some of his stress away.

>>> As a professor and a doctor, there is a reward of satisfaction in students remembering items taught to them that last a lifetime. Saving lives is a rewarding experience and the working days are never the same two in a row. Drawbacks are that no matter where you are, if people know you're a doctor they tell gross medical problems to you while you're trying to enjoy a meal.

MARITAL PROBLEMS

After the "big three" parental problems—money, teenage children, and jobs—came relationships and partners (spouses, boyfriends, girlfriends, "significant others") and the stresses of divorce. More than one-third of the papers mentioned such problems, and there is really no way to know how many parents might have felt that it was inappropriate to discuss such matters with a teen for a class interview.

One paper discussed the **loss of communication** which leads to marital problems.

>>> One person that I interviewed said the main personal problem adults go through is losing communication with their spouse, which leads into marital problems. This person gave me some examples that cause marital problems, such as two adults getting involved with their work which takes time away from each other. Another example is, if their job consists of traveling, that keeps them away from home. This causes a lot of marriages not to work out because of too much time away from each other.

Marital problems may also be related to **finances and children.**

>>> Marital problems begin with financial or job problems, because anger develops. Teenagers also cause problems, for marriage clashes in raising a child cause people to see how different they really are. Some people realize, after they have three kids, that they're not right for each other, which in my opinion is a bit too late! Because they stay together for the kids, the longer they stay together the farther they grow apart.

Divorce creates a new relationship with society, family, and close relatives that can be especially difficult to adjust to.

>>> When you're married there are problems and if you're divorced there are problems. The woman I interviewed is divorced so she has to do a lot of things on her own. Another problem is since she has three kids she has to see her ex-husband quite a lot, which can be difficult at times.

>>> Another big problem or worry of hers is social pressure. She feels that it is very hard to try to go out with men because they figure that since she has been married before that she is ready to be sexually intimate with them right away.

>>> My mom loves [her new boyfriend] a lot, but my sisters dislike him. They dislike my mom and him being together and it really upsets my mom, and she gets really distressed.

>>> The loneliness syndrome is also a big problem. Being separated from husbands because of personal problems is very sad. One of these parents got separated from her husband because they couldn't stand each other and that led to a pain in her home.

THE FUTURE

Concern for the future was very closely connected with money, teenagers, and marital issues. Some parents expressed this in their **fear of loneliness,** which was also associated with children maturing and leaving the home—

>>> Adults fear the thought of being alone. After the children leave, adults sometimes feel insecure about their marital status. In some marriages the children are the only reason the parents stay together. And if you are a single parent it can be worse....Most of their life they always had their children. When they move out and are

no longer dependent on that parent the parent seems less loved by the children. This is a case of growing old alone. And most single parents are afraid of that idea.

>>> The mother I talked to said that she was having troubles accepting the fact that her children are growing up. She realizes there is going to be a time when she has to say goodbye but it will be very hard.

—with the **loss of parents and other loved ones:**

>>> His most prominent personal problem is the "thought of losing loved ones." This thought is painful to everyone, but especially to him. He thinks about this subject often because his father recently passed on. His mother and uncle are aged, and he frequently worries about them.

—and with the thought of **growing old:**

>>> The man I talked to has many personal problems. He worries about old age and wonders "Where will I be?"

Other concerns for the future were expressed as well. Some parents even **worried about worrying.**

>>> The last problem these people found to be of great importance was worrying. Their worry was caused by bills, and one or two even worried about worrying. One person was scared and worried about what will happen to their marriage AFTER the children were grown and gone. Some would try to hide their problems, like money or jobs, from their children, and thus became worried about that. One person said he was scared of getting old and another of a nuclear war and what they and their family would do in such a holocaust.

In all, the Parent/Teen Book Group found that in 14 of the 36 papers, parents expressed concern over the future. We considered calling this section "Stress" and including parents' references to bad situations that they imagined *could* exist but that didn't really exist at the moment—all those "worries about worries," in other words. Why didn't we? When we started counting, we didn't know where to stop.

SOCIAL CONCERNS

One last category of parental issues we labeled "Social Concerns." There were a few references to nuclear war, world affairs, crime and drugs, and social morality. The economy was also mentioned, but always in the context of personal concerns—over money, jobs, Social Security, and inflation.

Although few, these references stood out in contrast to the other problems. One man, for example, showed his concern about fulfilling his proper role in and **feeling a part of society.**

>>> He said also that another large problem is keeping up with the increase in productivity and keeping up with information about what's going on in the world, in the United States, in our state, and with the government. He worries that he doesn't know enough to make the right decisions when voting for the president or governor, or for any of the propositions.

But by far the most eloquent expression of social concern was the following paper. It demonstrates a global perspective on the part of the parents and was unlike any other paper written for the assignment.

>>> ECONOMY, EDUCATION, COMMITMENT

I interviewed two adults, my father and my stepmother. In both interviews the information was much the same. I take this to mean these are important issues, as the viewpoints seem to enforce one another. However, it is possible that these adults share the same views be

cause they are close to one another. In these interviews I found three major problems adults have today.

The first major problem, identified in both interviews, is economic issues. Both said that adults are concerned about housing. They want a good house and affordable payments. These are affected along with taking care of a family by job availability. This, in turn, is affected by governmental leadership and policies which can change the whole economic system.

The second major problem, mentioned in my first interview, is that people have become apathetic in their ties to the world. Although technology has increased our potential for communication dramatically, adults gradually seem to be losing the ability to communicate person to person. This person feels that "people can't make meaningful utilization of data" because education is lacking. Instead of hands-on experience and training, today's education seems to be centered on the use of outside sources and services. As this person put it, "We have become a nation of observers, accustomed to being entertained, rather than creating and participating in our own entertainment."

The final problem I discovered was brought up by both of the people I interviewed. It can be summarized as lack of commitment. This is seen in many situations. First of all, in the workplace, there is a shift in the work ethic. Everyone wants a job, but no one wants to work too hard. Lack of commitment is also seen in the high divorce rate. People expect wonders, and then they want to get out if trouble arises. It is seen in the parents who send their kids to school every day and then get a babysitter every night. This basic lack of commitment and responsibility is one of the major underlying problems of adult society today.

In conclusion, let me first say that adults face many problems today, but I believe that those mentioned above are among the most important because they permeate all other aspects of society. Government leadership affects prices, interest rates and employment, but it also runs much deeper than that. That waffle you ate for breakfast contained only government certified goods, and so on. The lack of person-to-person communication can be seen everywhere, from our relationships with our family and friends to the relations between governments. The lack of hands-on training is obvious in most businesses. The lack of commitment is seen in shorter people-to-people, people-to-jobs, and government-to-government relations. There is no easy solution to these problems, but with better education during youth, they might be lessened. In this, at least, youth can share the responsibility with adults.

AN EYE-OPENER

The parents quoted in this chapter were honest and thoughtful about describing their problems to their teenage interviewers. The students were impressed by the variety of problems that these parents faced and the courage with which they revealed themselves to teenagers. The assignment also brought up another question: How often do teens, in daily life, actually ask adults how they are doing, or what is bothering them? Many parents were clearly relieved to "unload" and share their frustrations and fears with someone. Almost all of them had money problems, and many had worries about their teens. Most were under stress in one form or another. Some had marital or extramarital problems, many were worried about their future, a few were even concerned for the future of our nation and our world.

For at least some of the teens who wrote these papers the assignment was an eye-opener. Here is what a few of them said:

>>> After hearing about the problems parents have, I begin to wonder if I'll have these same problems as an adult. After all, when you are just a teenager in high school, you don't really see what's going on in the world. After listening to these parents, I found myself thinking about how to prepare for when I get out of school and get a job. Doing this paper really opened my mind to a lot of questions about myself.

>>> I was aware of most of these problems except I didn't realize that adults have as much sexual pressure as teenagers do.

>>> Adults have just as many, if not more, problems than the average teenager. Through interviewing these two women I felt sympathy for them. I also discovered their problems are often more serious than mine at the moment. Since both women I talked with have the same type of problems, chances are mine will also be similar when I reach their age. I feel this assignment will be useful to me when I begin to make long-term decisions, by reflecting back on the problems of others.

>>> After interviewing two parents with teenage children I found out that they have just as many problems as their children. The parents' problems, however, are more serious and could affect the whole family. I also learned that as you get older more problems occur. It's hard for me to see how growing up changes people's lives. People become more concerned about things that had little importance when they were younger.

>>> Now I know that adults have problems too. They may seem strong on the outside. But most of the time they're not as strong on the inside. Teenagers don't seem to realize that parents have problems relating to them as well as they have problems relating to parents. I also learned that adults seem to become more insecure as they get older.

3

IF I WERE A PARENT

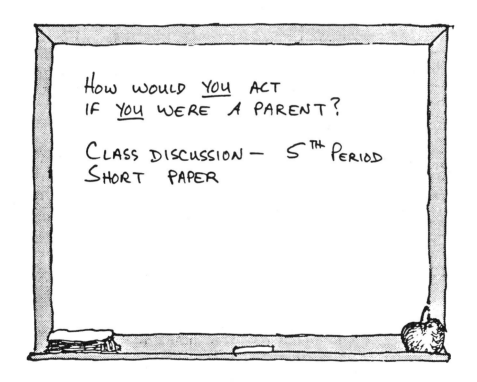

How would YOU act
if YOU were a parent?

Class discussion — 5TH Period
Short paper

JOEL: A DAYDREAM

Joel sat at his desk daydreaming about the girl at the desk behind him. In his mind he saw her and him in his '57 T-Bird, cruising down Central Avenue. He could almost see his friends' faces when he walked by with her on his arm, their envious stares and admiration. They'd take romantic walks on the beach at night, smelling the cool sea breeze and feeling the sand between their toes as the waves rolled in and out. They would spend carefree hours in town, without a worry in the world.

Eventually, Joel thought, they might even get married, have kids. He would go to college first, get a good job. They would have a boy and a girl. He'd give them the best, he'd be a great father—understanding, strict but fair. He wouldn't make the same mistakes his dad had made. . .

A piece of paper was slipped onto his desk. He looked down and groaned: He had an F on his Sex-Ed test.

This entire chapter is, in a sense, a daydream that the students were asked to have about how they would act when *they* became parents. While the students wrote their essays on teen and parent problems the English classes became almost like group therapy sessions. The students realized it was safe to discuss openly what they had written about. But some of the students were content to sit at the back of the class and complain about parents always saying things like "When I was your age," and laugh and groan and agree with one another.

It was time to think about solutions to the problems they were complaining about.

So in one class period the teacher asked the students to list *all* of the problems that existed between teens and parents. These were written on the blackboard until it was totally filled and looked like the one on page 59. She then asked the students to circle their personal "hot items"—the real sore spots, the BIG problem areas—and list them in order of importance. When the lists were complete, the students were told: "Refer to your list and write an essay describing how YOU would handle these concerns if you were the parent of teenage children."

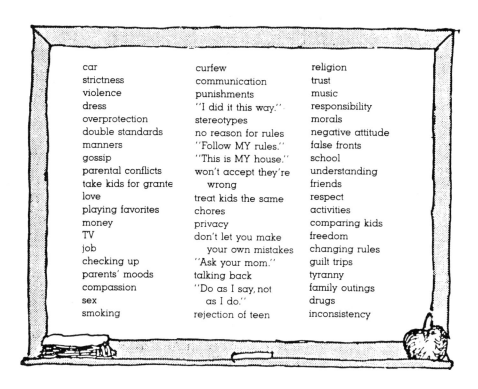

car	curfew	religion
strictness	communication	trust
violence	punishments	music
dress	"I did it this way."	responsibility
overprotection	stereotypes	morals
double standards	no reason for rules	negative attitude
manners	"Follow MY rules."	false fronts
gossip	"This is MY house."	school
parental conflicts	won't accept they're	understanding
take kids for grante	wrong	friends
love	treat kids the same	respect
playing favorites	chores	activities
money	privacy	comparing kids
TV	don't let you make	freedom
job	your own mistakes	changing rules
checking up	"Ask your mom."	guilt trips
parents' moods	talking back	tyranny
compassion	"Do as I say, not	family outings
sex	as I do."	drugs
smoking	rejection of teen	inconsistency

While this essay was being written, the students were encouraged to discuss their ideas with each other, and the classes did an exercise in writing a list of rules for the household that are fair to everybody. (Those rules are presented in Chapter 4.) The whole idea boiled down to this: Turn gripes into positive solutions.

We would like to invite you, the reader, to circle your hot spots on the blackboard too. And while you certainly do not have to write an essay, if you are a teenager, you might stop for a minute and think about how you would handle these problems if you were a parent of teens. If you are an adult, and a parent, you might think about how you do handle these problems with your teens.

Forty-five papers were submitted, and each was very different. Generally, though, the solutions discussed seemed to fall into three groups, as shown below:

Positive goals

Communication	mentioned	22	times
Freedom/independence	"	22	"
Trust	"	16	"
Understanding	"	14	"
Responsibility	"	13	"
Privacy	"	12	"
Respect	"	7	"

Specific, day-to-day issues

Punishment	mentioned	12	times
Moral decisions	"	6	"
School	"	5	"
Curfew, money	"	3	"
Chores, friends	"	2	"
Sex, driving, music, sports, smoking/drugs, fair rules, activities, second marriage	"	1	time

Negative behavior and attitudes

Double standards	mentioned	6	times
Guilt trips, overprotection, inconsistency	"	5	"
Comparing kids	"	4	"
Favoritism	"	3	"
Religion	"	2	"
Tyranny, rejection of teen, violence, taking others for granted, parent-parent conflict	"	1	time

The following paper is typical of many of the students' concerns. On the whole, it is also representative of the "positive" issues listed above.

>>> RESPONSIBILITY, INDEPENDENCE, MORALITY, AND COMMUNICATION

Many teenagers today feel that they never want to become parents. I, however, would really like to become a parent some day, and maybe the ideas and views I have now won't be the same then, but right now I feel four major concerns would be responsibility, independence, morality, and communication.

I feel responsibility is a very important quality, and one in which I hope my children will gain when I become a parent. Responsibility is something that can be taught by the parents, or adults, but the final action is up to the person himself. Learning this can mean anything from being responsible for their own actions, to being concerned for others, or being on time somewhere, doing something they know has to be done, or accepting blame for something they know they did wrong. Sometimes it's not always easy to be responsible one-hundred percent of the time, and I wouldn't expect my children to be perfect, but if I felt they were responsible it would make it easier for me to trust them.

I also feel trust is an important factor in bringing up children, but the hardest part is knowing how much trust and responsibility to give them. If I really trusted my child, and he kept deceiving me, it would make it hard for me to trust him and some of his privileges would be taken away. Constantly being untrustworthy, I feel is not responsible behavior, and I surely hope I can set a good example of responsible behavior to my children.

Independence is another area which must be learned by the individual. Some children have more independence than others, but I feel in order for a person to grow emotionally, they need to have a certain amount. This becomes most evident during the teenage years but quite often it appears early in childhood. Sometimes parents would like their children to have the same views or ideas about things as they have, or they

would like to see them become just like they are, or something they themselves weren't. I feel it is extremely important for a child to feel his or her own sense of identity. I would try to the best of my ability to let my children have the certain amount of independence that they need, but I am also aware of how hard it is to let your child grow, especially as they're getting older, and they're growing more away from you. They need a time to separate their ideas and beliefs from their parents'. As a parent, I would then watch and learn from them, as hopefully they did from me.

I know one area that would be a little difficult, especially in bringing up teenagers, is morality. The morals that I have, or believe in, and had set for my family might not necessarily be what my child believes in. The major concerns I would have would be pressures from peers. I know from experience that sometimes what "everyone else is doing" might seem like the great thing to do, even if you don't feel it is right. I feel it would be my responsibility as a parent to teach my kids what I feel is right and wrong, and tell them about my own mistakes so maybe it can limit their amount of mistakes. Of course they will make mistakes, and probably not all our beliefs and values will be the same, but I just hope they won't make any big mistakes.

A final step which is probably the most important part of being a successful parent, and having a close, loving relationship with your family, is communication. Without communication there is nothing, at least the way I see it. It is the basis for everything. To me, it is so important to be able to talk about things, to praise for something good, but to show the right way if something wasn't right. It isn't always easy to communicate, and I know that very well, but with my children I would try my very best to keep the lines of communication open, and hear how they feel, as well as tell them how I feel. One of the things I hate the most is when one of my parents tunes me out, and refuses to listen to what I have to say, even if they know I'm right. If I knew I was wrong, and my children were right, although I know it wouldn't be easy, I'd really try to admit to it.

Maybe as I grow older I'll find these areas harder to deal with, and maybe these things won't be as important to me. I'll just try and be the best parent I can be, because I don't believe there is such a thing as a "perfect parent." I only hope I can raise my children to be responsible, have independence, high morals, and that I'll be able to communicate with them.

The writer of this paper has obviously thought a great deal about the broader aspects of parenting. Other teens were more literal about what they would do in certain situations.

>>> RULES, TRUST, INDEPENDENCE, AND PRIVACY

A parent goes through a lot raising a child. They have to take care of them until they are old enough to be on their own. A parent has to set certain rules and stick to them. A child must follow these rules or be punished for disobeying them. A parent and his child can get along

great and have no problems if a child follows certain responsibilities, has a good bond of trust with his parent, and has a certain amount of independence and privacy.

A parent sets many restrictions on certain privileges a child has. It is the child's responsibility to obey them and not abuse them. Curfew is probably the most important one. If the child is supposed to be home before 10:00 every night and is late he should be punished. A child should also have a responsibility to help around the house and clean up after himself.

Trust is a very important part of a relationship between a parent and his child. A parent should be able to trust his child to tell the truth to him all the time. A parent should set certain rules and trust his child to obey them. A child should trust his parent to be honest and fair with him. When a parent lets his child borrow the car he should trust him not to wreck it or mess around in it.

A very important thing to a child is independence. Teens like to be free and be able to go places with their good friends. A parent has to respect his child's independence. A parent should let his child go places with his friends. The parent should let his children be alone for a while to think about their problems. Independence is a good thing to have.

A parent can have an easier life and a good relationship with his child if he raises them right and the child obeys his parents' rules. Trust, responsibility, independence, and a certain amount of privacy are three things that will make a relationship between a parent and his child stronger.

The first paper is very idealistic and abstract; the second seems more practical, issue-oriented, and yet, in its own way, is also idealistic. Read together, their different tones, their different points of view, say a lot about how individual we are. They bring out clearly that there is no single set of ideas or actions that can be called "right parenting," and yet there is something like a common view: enlightened and informed, firm and fair, with consideration on both sides.

In the next paper, even more specific than the last two, the writer is basically reacting as a teen to the mistakes he feels his parents have made, while at the same time struggling to carve out his or her own, improved, parental role.

>>> SET RULES AND STANDARDS

Parents have a very hard life. They have to set the rules and standards for their child to live by. These standards should be fair to everyone. The rules should also be strict, so that the child doesn't "walk" on the parents.

If I were a parent, I would try not to forget how hard it is being a child. Many parents put a great deal of stress on the child's work at school. I would not "make" my kid get good grades. Although it is nice to have good grades, I wouldn't punish him for getting poor grades, as long as I knew he tried his best.

Many fathers try to force their children to get involved in sports. I think that this is wrong. If the child wants to be in sports, he should be allowed to. I was forced into joining sports and I hated it. I don't feel that parents have the right to make their child do something not necessary.

There are many responsibilities in and around the house. If I were a parent, I would try to divide the chores fairly between the family members. I would try not to put too many responsibilities on my child. If I did give him too much responsibility, he would probably acquire a "mental block" against housework as he got older. I wouldn't give my child chores that are beyond his capabilities either. This would, more than likely, just frustrate him and this frustration would probably make him quit his chore.

I would let my child have privileges as long as he proves that he is worthy of them. A few of these privileges are curfew, dating, and going places. If he abuses these privileges, I will take them away from him until he can respect them.

Many parents give their children allowances. After their children get jobs, they take away the allowance. I would not do this if I were a parent. This would make the child feel independent too fast. The child might think that the parent is trying to "make" him feel less dependent. This would cause many fights and conflicts between the parents and child.

Sooner or later, my child will want to become independent. When this time comes, I will do as my parents did. They set down the rules and let me do as my independent mind wanted to do—as long as it didn't break any rule.

In a way, I can't wait to be a parent. But yet, I can. Being a parent is a hard job to do. A child's life depends on what one or two people feel is "right and wrong."

"Being a parent is a hard job to do." It must be, since "a child's life depends on what one or two people feel is 'right and wrong.' " The last two lines of that essay seem to capture the whole struggle that goes on in families, a struggle about giving and taking and each side wanting to do it in their own way.

The next student went into even greater detail about how her mother has raised her, and how she would handle her own teenagers differently.

>>> FOR THE GOOD OF THE TEEN

In today's world, teenagers are faced with parental problems that affect them throughout their lives. Most teenagers seem to have an overwhelming resentment for their parents and the decisions they make concerning them. They tend to believe that they would solve problems in a totally different manner. However, the decision a parent makes is usually for the good of the teenager.

One of the biggest problems between my parents and I is religion. My mother feels that she should force me to go to church, choose my religion, pick the kind of music I listen to, and many other things like this concerning our religion. Personally, I think it is wrong. If I believe in God it should be because I want to, not because I would get grounded if I don't. I plan on letting my kids choose whether or not they will become religious. I will try and guide them towards it but never force it on them.

Other problems are the moral standards my mother sets for me. She treats me the same way she was thirty years ago. If it wasn't proper to do something then, then to her it isn't proper to do it now. There are things I can't do because it wouldn't be proper for a girl my age to go there and to come home at a late hour. This conflicts with my social life and work since I'm scheduled late hours. I feel that a curfew should be no earlier than 11 P.M. on weekends and 10 P.M. on weekdays. I should be able to go out and work during the week as long as it doesn't interfere with school.

As with all families, punishments seem to always create confrontation between parents and teenagers. Many times it is the question as to if the teenager should be let off without punishment, and if there is to be a punishment what it should be. One thing for sure is that I would always give my kids a second chance. If they did it again a light punishment would be given. After the next time, the punishment would get more and more severe.

A big problem that has risen in the teenage society is freedom. They just seem to want to be free of their parents and be out on their own. I don't think teenagers should have total freedom because they need some guidance from their parents. If a teenager has lack of freedom then they are confined to friends with the same restrictions. Therefore, girls as well as guys find it quite difficult to accomplish tasks by themselves because they have become dependent on their parent because of lack of freedom.

Communication is also a big problem. Because of lack of communication relationships between parent and teenager aren't good. They don't talk so they don't understand why the other is the way he or she is. There are just some things that can't be talked about because arguments may start. When I'm a parent, I hope that my children and I can talk about anything and still keep a peaceful relationship.

However hard it is to keep a good relationship with your parents, you should try your best. Sometimes it seems to me like I'm the only teenager with these problems. I know now that many are faced with the same problems as me and their parents seem to handle situations sort of like my parents do. When I'm a parent I hope to make things easier for my kids than they are for me now by looking back on how things were when I was a teenager.

Strong contradictions surface in this paper. At the beginning, the writer says that parents usually make decisions for the good of the teen, yet it is clear from the rest of the essay that she does not really think so, at least not in her own case.

The next paper discusses two issues that were specifically mentioned only in this paper: The essay suggests how a stepparent should discipline his children; it also discusses sex.

>>> TREAT THEM WITH THE SAME RESPECT

If I were the parent and I had two children, I would treat them with the same respect they treat me. Neither one of the children would be any better than the other. If one had to wait until she was sixteen to date, so would the other.

If I had been divorced at one time or another, I would adjust to the way my new husband disciplined children, but he would have to adjust to my ways too. The children should be allowed to see the rest of their family on any vacation time.

When the children do something wrong, they will be punished in some way, shape or form. The punishment will fit the crime. For instance, if they're late getting home and don't have any good reason at all, then they'll be put on restriction the next weekend when they want to go out.

Their curfew will vary. Before they're sixteen, they can double date and go out with their friends, and they'll be home by ten. When they're sixteen, they can date a boyfriend and stay out until twelve. Like I said, if they're late without reason, they'll be punished.

When it comes to music, I believe they should be able to listen to whatever they want just so long as they don't "blast the house down." I'm sure in time, they'll grow out of styles of music as the fads change. I know I did.

Sex is a completely different story. I really feel that at the age of sixteen most kids are emotionally ready for something like that. But then again, some aren't. I would definitely have to talk with them about sex and see how they feel about sex, and about what they think it will do for them and their relationship with their boyfriend.

I would always try to be as open and as honest a parent as possible. Sure, there will be times when I'll have to hide the truth about something from them, but it would only be for their own good. I would just like to have a close relationship with them in hopes that they won't hide things from me. I would want my kids to grow up with respect for honesty and I don't want them to think that life is one big bowl of cherries.

Now I'm not saying that I'd be the best parent in the world, but I would definitely try. There will be bad times and good times of course, but I would try to make every good thing in life memorable for my children.

The paragraph on sex in the paper above is an example of the kind of uncertainty on serious issues that many of the papers contained. The writer starts out strong— "I really feel that at the age of sixteen most kids are emotionally ready for something like that"—then follows with "But then again, some aren't." Clearly the teen is trying to take in contradictory views and find a middle ground. It is not an easy task, and the essay expresses a lot of the ambivalence and contradiction many parents also feel.

Perhaps the effort to "daydream" a parental role for themselves can help teens to understand the tension created in parents when they hold opposing viewpoints and must come up with a single, "right" answer. Parents, too, may find in these essays mirrors that reflect what kind of parents they are. They also point to some areas where today's parents, perhaps even more than their teens, need to rethink their own values and behavior.

Almost as though to contradict all this, the next paper

presents a very strict attitude toward raising teens. The writer has resolved all her ambivalence and doubts and replaced them with RULES.

>>> LOVE, PATIENCE, UNDERSTANDING—AND RULES

If I were a parent, I would try to raise my children to the best of my ability. There are quite a few things I would do in order to accomplish this, while making sure that while I did this, it was done with love, patience, and understanding.

In my home, I would set down some rules. Supposing my children are teenagers, I would start by telling them my three main rules followed by any smaller ones. The first rule would be respect for parents as well as others and their property. This means using the golden rule in all your dealings with people. The next rule would have to be that they keep strong in church and school activities—to accomplish all they could. The third would be—Do as they are asked at all times. I would explain that as a parent, I had lived longer, knew more, and I know what's best for them. I would follow this with smaller rules concerning chores, grades, etc. Then I would proceed to tell them the consequences if they disobeyed these rules. If they failed to do what was expected of them, I would take away privileges such as dating, visiting friends, or using the car.

When it comes to favoritism I would be sure to make it quite clear that I loved all the children the same so as to discourage jealousy which leads to sibling rivalry. I would balance each child's work and play according to what each child could handle. Obviously larger jobs and more responsibility would deserve more privileges than smaller jobs. All the children would be treated the same. Their sex would have nothing to do with their curfew. Again, I would remind them of the Golden Rule in their treatment of each other, and the consequences of fighting.

School is quite an important issue also, mostly because it teaches responsibility and gives children a chance to do well in life later. I would stress this to my children and tell them the other benefits such as more privileges. As with the other rules or responsibilities there would have to be punishment if they neglected to do this job.

Last of all, the social life of children would play an important part of parenthood. After all, the definition of parenthood is the socialization of children. Therefore, they would have to get out in order to accomplish this. But there are certain limits to be set and my main task is to teach my children responsibility so they can get by in life. So this category springs from the same thing as all the rest: their privileges are given according to their obedience to the household rules.

I think I would make a good parent if I used these rules and ideas as a guide to raising my children.

A PANDORA'S BOX OF PARENTAL NO-NO'S

The paragraph on favoritism in the paper above is an example of an issue categorized earlier in this chapter as a "Negative," a parental behavior the teens hoped to avoid. What follows is a sampling of what other teens had to say about other Negatives.

Comparing Kids

Comparing children is also a big wrong! When one asks or tells his child, "Why aren't you like your brother?" or "Why are you doing this? Your brother didn't," it only makes the child feel as if he has to be in someone else's shoes and not in his own. The child should feel he can grow up as himself, not worrying about impressing others.

Overprotection

Overprotecting the child won't be beneficial to the child in the future. Overprotection and constantly "looking out for" him will make the child seem different from others his own age. I believe children should be able to experiment on their own and learn by their own mistakes. A parent won't always be able to stand up for them. Often a child who has been overprotected all his life will grow up paranoid or unable to enjoy life because of the lack of opportunity to get out without parents with him. Overprotection eventually will leave a child feeling lonely and unhappy.

Double Standards

I also think parents should listen to what they say and practice what they preach. I think a lot of parents yell at their children and tell them not to do certain things yet they do them themselves and I don't think that is right.

Inconsistency

Another mistake parents make is inconsistency. An example of inconsistency is when your mom says, "This is

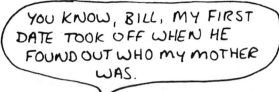

my house, my car," and then the next day says, "This is your house too, so do some work." I would tell my son if he does his work he will get a fair amount of use of the car and go places. But, if he doesn't, I will probably be inconsistent in some ways.

Guilt Trips

I am against the use of guilt trips, even though I sometimes employ them myself. They inspire a feeling of low self-worth, because they make a person feel that he is responsible for some wrong. Guilt can be a powerful tool, but it almost always hurts those who are involved, through self-doubt and the weakening of relationships.

Tyranny

Tyranny in a family can cause uproars of all kinds. I feel that a household containing any kind of tyranny is usually an unhappy household. When a family feels pressures due to one family member, communication is no longer at hand. When the child in the family feels this power, he usually begins to feel helpless and weak. Soon the child is unwilling to communicate due to his fear of being punished. Because I am such an open person and I believe in good communication between people, I find myself very against this kind of activity. If a parent starts out being open with his child, problems such as tyranny would most likely be more uncommon.

Favoritism

Letting my children know I love them the same, no matter what, has always been important to me. I hate it when parents have favorites, so I doubt I will. Many kids think they get punished because "Mommy and Daddy don't love me" or "They love him/her more than me." With the way I feel about that, I might have a lot of explaining to do. I'd feel terrible if one of my children felt less loved than the other(s) because of how I treat him or her.

LET THE CONSEQUENCE FIT THE CRIME

One of the Negatives that we would like to handle separately is **punishment** or, as it is more often called these days, **consequences.** It was given at least a paragraph in twelve out of the forty-five papers and was mentioned in numerous others. Here is an example of a "hard line" on punishment:

>>> I will punish my child if need be. He/she will not get away with murder! I will not be blind and say, "Well, my little Johnny did that?" My child will probably be spoiled but he/she will be punished! When they are small they will be spanked. When they get to the age of thirteen, privileges will be taken away! Such as the telephone, the television, and RESTRICTION!!!!!

Many of the other teens said punishment should not be too severe:

>>> I must warn both teens and parents that too many times a punishment is carried out that is too severe for the "crime," so to speak. I am warning teens too, because

they also can punish their younger brothers and/or sisters. I know what it feels like to be whipped or spanked. The hardest thing to do is not to punish somebody the way a parent may have been punished. So what I'm trying to say is be careful, and don't overdo. It could cause more problems than do good.

Teens also thought that it is important to know the consequences of one's actions. Punishments should be consistent.

>>> Dealing with the punishments of my children will definitely be different from what I've known. I will be consistent and not let big wrongs slide by. They will be punished for something they've done wrong as soon as it is known to me and not a week after. Their restrictions will be fair to all and not cruel nor unusual. They will all get the same punishment for the same wrong and no one will get off any easier than the other did.

AND, ON A HAPPIER NOTE, . . .

In this chapter, we have reproduced in full six out of forty-five papers written on the topic, "If I Were a Parent." Some were abstract, others were very specific. Many tried hard to offer honest and realistic solutions to some of the problems touched on in the first two chapters of this book. The one below, however, comes close to saying it all.

>>> FIVE GOOD IDEAS ABOUT RAISING TEENAGERS

Raising children, whether they are young children or teenagers, is a very difficult responsibility, which is why some adults regard it as a lifetime job. And when it does come time for me to take my turn as a parent I, like everyone else, will try my hardest to do what's right for both my children as well as for me.

I believe that violence is wrong at any age; therefore I will do everything I can to prevent it in my own home. I will not punish my children by hitting them nor will they be allowed to hit each other.

Communication is another idea that I would like to mention. I want my children to feel free to discuss anything with me just as I want to be able to discuss anything with them. I think that openness plays a very important part in the relationship between parents and children. Once this openness goes away between me and my son or daughter I will treat them more like children than young adults.

Morals are also something that I feel very strongly about. I think parents should teach their children right from wrong, such as: sex is wrong any time out of marriage, and lying is wrong all the time.

The last idea I want to get across is the amount of compassion that goes on in my family. I want to always be able to hug my children without them feeling weird or awkward, just as I want them to feel easy about hugging me when they want, without feeling strange.

In conclusion I want to stress that I will do anything I have to do to keep my children feeling good about themselves. I want them to grow up and remember us as being friends.

Someday, sometime, you too may want to list "Five Important Ingredients for Raising Teenagers." Whether you are a parent now or a parent-someday-to-be, we hope "compassion" and a few hugs make it onto your list.

And now, turn to Chapter 4
to have some fun
With Rules to Live By
that are FAIR TO EVERYONE

4

RULES TO LIVE BY
THAT ARE FAIR
TO EVERYONE

RULES TO LIVE BY
— THAT ARE FAIR TO EVERYONE —

1. _____   6. _____
2. _____   7. _____
3. _____   8. _____
4. _____   9. _____
5. _____   10. _____

LIST, THEN WRITE SHORT PAPER —
DUE FRIDAY !

SHEILA AND HER FATHER: TWO SCENARIOS

Sheila

I'm a sixteen-year-old girl. My dad just divorced my mother and married a great lady named Janice.

Life with my mother was tough. She was very strict with me and my brother Rand; teens were to be seen, not heard. But my father and I could really talk to each other. He told me how bad my mother had it and that I should try to understand her, but I could tell that he didn't understand her either. Then my mother started to try to run my father's life. She bothered him about his job, not enough money, too many meetings—the list goes on.

My father didn't need a second mother. He needed more support than my mom gave him. That's where Janice came in. She gave him all the care and love he needed, so he divorced my mother and married Janice.

I hated Janice at first. I was afraid we'd get stuck with the same rules our mother laid on us. My brother and I might not always get along, but we were ready to fight Janice if we had to. When she asked us to talk to her, to help her work out a set of house rules, I almost died! We did it, but I still wonder if it will all work out.

Her Father

I'm a thirty-seven-year-old man. I have just married Janice, my second wife. I finally realized that I never fully understood my first wife, and that we really didn't know each other after being married for eighteen years. I felt that she wanted too much out of me, when all I asked for was a little support.

My two kids, Rand, seventeen, and Sheila, sixteen, were always fighting with each other and with their mother and me. My daughter told me how strict she thought her mother was, but I still couldn't give her all the freedom she wanted. I worried about Sheila, about all those things you read in the paper and hear on the news, but I tried to give her as much freedom as I could. I was more lenient with Rand, because he is older and better able to take care of *himself. But they were never quite satisfied; they always wanted to do something new, and they always had an argument ready. I was afraid that bringing in someone new would only make things worse, and things were a little bit rocky at first. But this evening, when I walked in from work, I found the three of them all sitting in the living room, making a list of rules to live by. It sounded great, but still, I'm worried. Will it all work out?*

Raising teenagers, parents often worry about how things will turn out: "Will my teenager be alright if I say yes to that overnight beach party? Should I let him drive the truck? If I do, am I being too lenient? If I don't, is that being overprotective? Where do I set the limits? And what's fair to *me*? I need the truck next weekend, too. After all, I paid for it!"

Teens wonder and worry, too: "Dad knows everyone who's going. Why won't he trust me? I've never had an accident. He wants me to be grown up and do my chores and homework on my own, but he doesn't think I'm ready to have fun on my own. When will Dad stop treating me like a baby? It's not fair!"

What *is* fair is the subject of this chapter. For a classroom assignment the teens were asked to create a list of "Rules to Live By That Are Fair to Everyone." Later, the Parent/Teen Book Group asked parents to make their own list of rules. The assignment was not as easy as it may sound, and you or your family may want to try it. Ten was the recommended number of rules, but you don't need to limit yourself.

Unlike Chapter 3, which offered ideas for how teen-parent relationships could be and should be in a happy future, this chapter deals with solutions for the present. The need to define workable rules resulted in well-focused and down-to-earth responses.

The first section deals with three pairs of themes, starting with respect and rights, which underlie most rules, such as those about understanding, privacy, and sharing. Honesty and trust come next, followed by responsibility and freedom. The next section contains rules about the nitty-gritties of daily living: rules about school, curfew, use of the car and phone. The last section is about discipline—what to do when rules are broken.

Teen rules are given first, followed by parent rules, and there are many different opinions. We did not try to weed out repetition or contradiction: many voices contributed to this chapter, and our idea is to show the variety and the intensity of their concerns. There is no single "right" set of rules that will apply for every family, every situation, every cultural and social group; these rules are "solutions" only so far as they help all of us to see and think for ourselves and understand others.

Some rules relate to specific teen or parent gripes. Some may sound "hard-nosed," others show extreme leniency—all depending on your point of view. Many show a great deal of maturity on the part of the teens, and a plea for some recognition of this from their parents:

>>> Parents should listen to what is on our minds without interrupting or accusing.

Some rules point up serious problems about how to handle new and evolving family and social situations:

>>> I should be allowed to say whether or not I will go to my dad's. I am old enough now to make the decision on whether or not I'll go to stay with him.

And some are downright amusing. For example, one parent wrote:

>>> Set your own alarm clock.

>>> Turn off your electric blanket in the morning.

Yet, no matter how humorous a rule may seem, it is obvious that if someone goes to the trouble to write rules about electric blankets and alarm clocks, it is an area of friction in at least one household.

GROUND RULES #1: RESPECT & RIGHTS

Respect seems to be the basis for much of what follows in this chapter. If a teen doesn't show respect, the parent will not feel that the guidance and love he is offering is being appreciated. If the parent doesn't respect the teen, then the teenager is less likely to listen to his parent or follow the advice offered or the rules laid down.

From the teens
> Teenagers shall respect and take care of parents' property.
> Teenagers will respect their parents' feelings.
> Teenagers must not snap back at their parents; they must show an adult attitude if they wish to be treated like adults.
> Sometimes it's hard to give the parent credit when it is due. Ditto for the parents toward the teen. Try.
> Parents should believe in what we say.
> I shouldn't get nagged at all the time for how I walk or talk or even how I do my laundry. I am who I am and it should just be accepted. It's not like I'm messy or anything. It's just that I get yelled at for everything.
> Parents must not nag about little things that don't matter.

From the parents
> Respect each other's rights.
> Respect each other's needs.
> Treat people the way you want to be treated.
> Teen and parent will speak to each other with respect.
> Respect laws, adults, and guests.

> Don't interrupt when someone else is talking.
> Don't hit other people.
> Good language—no cussing.
> Do not answer parents back.
> Respect each other's property.
> Ask permission of the owner before using property.

PRIVACY

One obvious sign of respect is the respect of privacy. Both teens and parents need time alone to be themselves, to act as they want and think about what they feel. Parents mentioned specific violations of privacy—the mail, the phone. For teens, the bedroom is a sanctuary. And for both parents and teens, closed doors are to be respected.

From the teens
> If your son's (daughter's) room door is closed, you must knock and wait for an answer. If there is no answer, you will not enter.
> Parents will not be so nosy and have to know everything that's going on.

From the parents
> Don't invade someone else's room or messages or anything.
> Do not open each other's mail.
> Privacy and quiet times are needed—for everyone.
> Respect the privacy of others (phone, mail).
> Bedrooms are private but kept neat.
> Respect closed doors.

SHARED TIME

For the family to work as a unit, parents and teens also need to spend time together. And at least some of it should be "quality" time—time allowed for one another instead of time watching TV. Both teens and parents felt that this time should be planned and at the convenience of everyone.

From the teens

> Every night, take fifteen minutes at least to discuss any problems.
> Make time on certain days to spend just talking with us.
> Come to us when we're not busy.
> Everyone should get to have his or her say.

From the parents

> Parents and teenagers need to set aside time each week for the sole purpose of talking and sharing.
> Eat dinner at the same time each night with your family. Dinner conversation should be positive.
> One day every week or so we do something as a family.

UNDERSTANDING

During family time teens need to feel free to talk of their problems and their joys. They want and need understanding from their parents and think that parents should be open and able to listen without getting angry.

From the teens
> Parents and children should talk to one another more and try to understand why they feel differently about certain things.
> Listen to us when we are talking.
> Parents should listen to what is on our minds without interrupting or accusing.
> Teenagers should be able to talk to their parents openly about anything without feeling guilty or getting jumped on about their problems.
> Understand our problems and help.
> Parents should understand and accept their teenager as a person.

And the parents often need this communication too, not just to learn what the teens are thinking, but to receive some comfort themselves. Both teens and parents are looking for a common ground for communication.

From the parents
> When someone has a problem, they talk it out.
> When someone is talking, stop what you are doing and listen.
> Good relationships require a commitment to communication.
> When a disagreement between parent and teen arises, each party should listen to the other side before getting angry.
> Problems can be resolved through communication.

> Let teens know that you love them and that they can come to you with any problem and that love will not change, even if you voice your disapproval.

GROUND RULES #2: HONESTY & TRUST

For this communication to be effective, parent-teen relationships must be based on honesty and trust. The parents want to know the truth of what's going on. The teen wants to be trusted.

From the teens
> Trust me to go certain places and not do anything wrong.
> If a child gives no reason for mistrust, a parent should not take it for granted that his son or daughter is "like all other teenagers."

From the parents
> Be honest—as to your whereabouts, where you are going.
> Parents and teens need to promise to be as honest as possible with each other.
> Trust teens until they give you a reason not to.
> If you are wrong, admit it.
> We are honest with each other.
> Be very honest with everyone.
> Be honest with your feelings.
> If you love each other, don't be afraid to show it and say it!

GROWTH

One teen and two parents wrote a rule about growth. Teens do not want to be restricted from the opportunity to grow — and neither do parents.

From the teen
> Parents will not try to hold their children back from growing.

From the parents
> Problems are really projects/opportunities for growth.
> Growth is a never-ending process, not just limited to teenagers.

Growth is possible only in the soil of these "basics": respect, trust, understanding, time together and time apart. Then parents can begin to allow their children the freedom—and the responsibilities—that come with growth.

GROUND RULES #3: RESPONSIBILITY & FREEDOM

One of the major barriers to understanding and growth is the very fact that teens are becoming adults. A parent cannot expect a child to assume the responsibilities of an adult. As the child gets older, however, his or her responsibilities increase. How many chores and other responsibilities should a teen take on? Teens know they should help in the everyday running of the household—that they should, for example, keep their rooms clean (or risk losing their privacy if the parent has to clean it). One teen said

> Help around the house as much as possible instead of watching TV

but many teenagers feel that they have been given more responsibility than they can handle and they want fairness in the way responsibilities are assigned:

> Parents will divide all chores equally among family members and make sure they get done.
> Mom will clean up her own messes.

More rules were written by both teens and parents about responsibility than about any other single issue. Here's what they had to say.

From the teens

> Children should have responsibilities, but parents should not give them too many.
> Teens should be responsible for a clean room and do a few chores, such as take out the trash, do the dishes, etc.
> The teen must keep his room to at least standard condition.
> Clean your room on Saturdays, but do it well. If you forget once, you'll be doing it every time it's messy.
> If the teenager does not eat at home or he isn't there all day, the parents shouldn't make the teenager do dishes.
> Help parents out with the dishes without getting upset about it.
> If you do what you are told to do and your chores, you can go places without a hassle.
> Take into consideration how much I already do. Between homework, school and dancing I don't have a lot of time.

> Let's compromise and settle on certain days when things are hectic at home or what I have to do isn't mandatory or very important, so I can stay at home and help out or just be with the family.
> Ask ahead of time when you need me to baby-sit for my little sister. This way it will be more convenient for all involved and I'll know whether to make plans or not. Ask nicely. Don't just tell me that I'm going to baby-sit.

From the parents
> Everybody shares household responsibilities, with no sexual discrimination.
> We help each other to make household chores fair to all.
> All teens are responsible for their own room, plus a few other chores to help parents.
> Do chores first before doing other things.
> Work on hobbies when chores are done.
> Keep room and clothes clean and neat.
> Pick up trash around the house, inside and out.
> Clean motor vehicles.
> Share responsibility for household articles.

> Share household chores in the house in which everyone lives—that includes fathers.
> If you mess it up, you clean it up.
> All family members share in keeping the family running—this means chores.
> Help keep everything in its proper place.
> Pick up your things.

① CLEAN

② STANDARD

③ NATIONAL DIASASTER AREA

> Everybody pulls their own weight.
> Everyone is responsible for his/her own behavior.
> Assume responsibility for the consequences of your actions.

Freedom, much desired by teens, is closely connected to responsibility. As one parent put it,

> Teenagers' "freedom" should be measured in relationship to how responsible they are. Parents need to judge this very carefully.

Teens, on the other hand, want (and need) to feel that they are at least in partial control of their lives. The teen rules below reflect the limitations each writer faces; all of the rules ask for greater self-determination.

From the teens

> Parents cannot tell teenagers what they can and cannot do with themselves. Example: If I want to shave half my head, the parent cannot say I can't.
> Your teenager shall not be forced to play a sport he does not wish to play, nor shall he be kept from playing a sport he wishes to play.
> Give me space to make my own decisions about things that relate to me or my life.
> I should be allowed to say whether or not I will go to my dad's. I am old enough now to make the decision on whether or not I'll go to stay with him.

From the parents

> Prepare yourself to be self-sufficient.
> Learn to be on your own.
> Allow everyone to have their own opinions.
> Give teens the freedom to make choices, but offer your input and guidance.
> Don't tell other people what to do as long as most of their decisions are sane enough. Make suggestions, but don't demand that those suggestions be followed.

The parents' rules sound as if parents desire freedom for their teens also, although those parents who are not enthusiastic about teenage freedom may have omitted any rules on this subject.

IN THE LAND OF THE "NITTY-GRITTIES"

Many of the teen and parent rules focused on specific issues—chores, the phone, who should set the alarm clock, etc. In fact, these "nitty-gritty," day-to-day matters are often a source of real conflict in households. Most households have stated rules like the ones below, whereas rules about abstract themes such as honesty and trust are usually assumed.

In reading what follows, some parents might find that some of the current household rules that they are taking for granted are considered unfair by their teens. For instance, the rule

> Parents shall not tell me what to do with my own earned money.

implies that currently the teen *is* being told what to do with his hard-earned cash, and he resents it. Many of the other rules in this section could be similarly eye-opening.

MONEY

Money was one of the hottest items in the teens' lists of rules. And it is easy to see why: Like many of the other items covered in this section (the phone, the car, curfew, etc.), money is directly related to independence.

From the teens
> Parents can't say no to a teenager who wants to work. If they do say no, they have to pay the teen-

ager as much as the job would have been paying.

> Money is the responsibility of the person who earns it, but they must at least be open to suggestions by other family members.
> Parents will pay teens a fair allowance only if they earn it.
> If your teenager works around the house, cooking, cleaning, etc., then, if you have the money, give him a weekly allowance. Explain to him that this allowance is all he gets until the next week, so he must make it last. It will give him responsibility.
> I should be given money if I baby-sit for a long time, and not just be taken advantage of. I watch my little sister all the time. Most things I do without being paid, but sometimes I need money too.
> Parents will lend you money for the big trips you go on, and once in a while to go out with your friends, only until you get a job! Then you're on your own.
> Money should be shared throughout the household. What's yours is mine, and what's mine is yours.

From the parents

> Financial agreements ought to be handled with the whole family, to eliminate misunderstandings.
> Teens should get an allowance for doing chores.
> Teens should have a summer job to learn the value of money. Maybe the reason that parents get upset is that they think the money is being wasted.
> Teens should spend money on good, usable items.

PHONE, MUSIC, AND TV

Living in a household with teens, many parents feel that they can never use the phone. And teens feel that they are always being yelled at to get OFF the phone. Although rules about the phone, music, and television showed no consensus, they did point up a major area of conflict for most teens and their parents.

From the teens
> No talking on the phone for over an hour.
> Teenagers can talk on the phone as late as they want, as long as they don't make noise.
> Parents should let their teenagers talk on the phone as late as they want, as long as the phone doesn't ring past 10 P.M.
> If the teenager has long-distance phone calls, then the teenager should pay for half of the bill and the parent can pay the other half.
> Get me my own telephone in my room with my own line. I agree to help pay for it.
> Music can be reasonably loud; it can be heard throughout the house.
> Music preference and volume are the choice of the listener, as long as it does not interfere with priorities of others in the family or the neighborhood.
> I should be able to listen to any music I want without being nagged that it is bad or satanic, especially when my parents don't know anything about it.
> I will try not to drive people crazy with the loudness of my music.
> We can be quiet by staying outside with the radio on low.
> TV (who watches what when) will be a compromise.

From the parents
> Be considerate about sharing the telephone.
> Limit phone calls to fifteen minutes.
> Take turns with the TV set.
> Teens may not waste many hours watching TV.

CURFEW

Rules about the phone point up the problems of living together when the teenager is home. The minute he or she steps out the door, a whole new situation arises. Teens want the freedom to go out when they desire and come in later than dark. The parents want their teens home on time, whatever that time is. If the teen can't make it home, they want her or him to call (probably one of the few times a parent is delighted to have his teen pick up the phone).

Some teens see the rationality of a curfew and the parents' desire to know where they are. And one teen wanted parity: Parents, too, must tell where they are going.

From the teens

> I should have a certain time I have to be home each night.
> Teens must be home at midnight.
> My new curfew is 12:30—no later. If something happens that I can't make it, I'll call.
> Teenagers should be in by 1:00 A.M.
> Everyone should come to an agreement about the curfew. Compromise.
> I will usually tell parents where I am and get home before too late.
> Teenagers will always go where they say they are going and make the curfew home in time.

- > Parents will allow me later nightly hours (not un-reasonably early in the morning) as long as they know where I am.
- > Anyone will be allowed to return to the house at any time, as long as they have told other family members when they will be returning, and they are very quiet.
- > Parents shall always tell me where they are going and when they'll be back.

... PARENTS SHOULD COME HOME ON TIME TOO...

From the parents
- > Be home on time.
- > Be home in time for meals.
- > Be home by midnight.
- > Call when you will be late.
- > Teens will call if they are going to be more than thirty minutes later than expected.
- > If the teens want to stay out past curfew, they should talk to parents before the event, and if there is a good reason for the request, another time can be agreed upon.
- > Tell parents where you're going and with whom and when you expect to return. Call if plans change.
- > We tell each other our whereabouts.

> Teens will be where they say they will be or ask permission to change plans.
> Let parents know where children are going.
> Let children know where parents are going.

DATES

The rules about curfew lead to the next topic: "Who is that boy/girl you're going out with?" Teenagers want freedom to see whom they wish, and if they are required to bring dates home to meet the parents, they want unconditional approval of their choices. Interestingly, dating can be just as painful for single parents as it is for teens. One sensitive teenager said:

> Any date, whether of the parent or the teenager, shall not be judged by family members.

From the teens
> I will bring a date in for my parents to meet before I even think of going out.

> Parents shall accept and try to get along with any boyfriend I bring home. They shall accept him and make him welcome in our home.
> Parents cannot say who I can go out with and who I can't.

From the parents
> Dates, parties, etc., are not allowed on school nights.
> There must be a parent at a party in a home.
> Bring dates home to meet parents.
> Don't have sex with anyone unless you are practicing birth control.

THE CAR

Curfews and dating often relate to using the car. The teens who wrote these rules were sixteen or seventeen and were in the process of getting their driver's licenses. For suburban teenagers in Southern California, a car is often the only escape from the house other than school. But no matter where they are growing up, all teenagers feel the need for "wheels," and most have felt restricted by their parents over the use of the car. For the parents, teenage driving evokes nightmares of emergency rooms, police stations, and skyrocketing insurance premiums.

From the teens

> The family car will be available to teenagers if the teenager is responsible, if he pays for his own gas, and if the parent has no need of the car.
> Parents shall allow me to drive both of their cars when they are not being used, and shall have faith in me while I am doing so.
> Let teenagers at the age of sixteen start driving, unless they just don't deserve to. The teenager will show that she or he is responsible enough by his or her attitude.
> Parents should not be too paranoid to let their son or daughter drive the car.
> If you still don't trust us to drive on our own, take the time to keep going with us 'til you do.
> No drunk driving is allowed.

From the parents

> Don't drive anyone's car without their OK.
> When the teen starts to drive, know it's a privilege the parent allows him and not his right, since the parent is responsible for him.
> No drinking and driving.

SCHOOL

Once back from a late-night date, the teen must face the reality of school, even when he feels half dead. For many parents, curfews and restrictions on dating and driving are all connected with the desire to have their teen perform well in school, do his or her homework on time, and get enough rest. Many parents feel it is a losing battle, but they fight it nevertheless. They realize that school is one of the few places where a teenager's performance can be measured. Some choose rules about school that are meant to be encouraging; others, threatening.

Teens have a varied response to the demands of school. Some teens promised to do all of their schoolwork and to study for tests; others wanted to be allowed to make decisions about school on their own.

From the teens

> I should go to school every day and do the work.
> I will do my best in school.
> I should do my homework before I go anywhere after school.
> Homework must be completed every day; I may do nothing if homework is not done.
> Parents should be more understanding about grades. A "C" isn't bad, and I shouldn't get yelled at because of it.

> Teenagers shall never have to be reminded to do homework.
> Teenagers should try their best to get good grades but shouldn't be grounded for slight dropping of grades.
> Teenagers should take grades seriously because good grades will pay off in the long run. So if punishment is needed, then that is the resort the parents will take.
> Parents shall continue to encourage me to get good grades, but never threaten me if I start to slip.
> If parents know we're trying in school, leave us to work at our own pace.
> Parents should say, "I want you to get good grades because I love you, so it's up to you if you do your homework."
> Don't put too much pressure on me about my grades.

From the parents
> In life there are certain ages when certain responsibilities are the norm. In teenage years education is one of the important tasks and priorities. That should be clear.
> Maintain at least a "C" average in order to have extra privileges.
> Teens should get passing marks at school.
> The teen is responsible for his schoolwork; he is expected to earn a grade point average commensurate with his ability. At our house a "C" is frowned upon unless the class is very difficult.
> Do homework when you get home from school.
> Complete homework before watching TV.
> Study for tests and finals.
> Parents and teens should figure out how many hours per day are needed for homework and then the teen should do it with no argument.

SMOKING, DRINKING, AND DRUGS

At school and elsewhere, teens face pressure about smoking, alcohol, and drugs. Although few rules were submitted on these issues, they are interesting for what they point up and what they leave out. Some of the assumptions—for example, the acceptance of smoking in the first teen rule *and* in the first parent rule; the assumption that teenagers drink alcoholic beverages—may upset some readers and not surprise others at all.

From the teens
> I can smoke outside with my father, not in my mom's car.
> I may have one or two beers at family gatherings but not with my friends, because that's dangerous.

> I may not take drugs, because it's wrong. (I want a flat-out rule, not garbage like showing me dumb articles.)
> Drugs are unacceptable except to cure a medical problem.
> Teenagers should feel that they can talk openly to their parents about sexual relations and drugs.

From the parents
> Wait until sixteen for permission to smoke.
> No drinking (or drugs, of course), and leave a party where others are drinking before it gets out of hand. I would prefer that my teen not stay at a party where there is any teen drinking, but can't be sure how to monitor this. He knows we do not allow teen drinking at our home and that he had better be careful where he is and be aware of the behavior of others. "You are known by whom you are with."

DRESS

Teens considered this to be important, while parents did not even mention dress. The following are all teen rules.

> Teenagers may dress, to an extent, in the style they wish.
> Teenagers may dress as they choose, except when they start to look like rag people.
> Give your teenager some slack in dress-up styles. Look around at all the other teenagers, and if you see that they're wearing the same thing, then obviously no one will laugh at your teenager, so don't worry. Be patient; they'll eventually grow out of it.
> The style of clothing changes almost every year, so don't nag about a dress code.
> Parents might not believe in some of the things I do as a teenager nowadays, but I can do it as long as it's moral and sane and I look nice, not scummy.

FRIENDS

Like dress, friends was an issue not mentioned by parents, although the teens had a fair amount to say about it.

> Teens should not hang around people who are a bad influence and get into trouble a lot.
> Parents have no right to criticize the friends of the teen, and likewise for the teens.
> Parents will take into consideration that I have common sense, and I know who to associate with and who not to.
> I don't usually hang out with too many insane people.
> Friends may be chosen by the teenager until it starts to affect the teenager's way of life.
> I should have the right to choose my friends. I believe I have good judgment.

SUPPORT AND ENCOURAGEMENT

Like dress and friends, support and encouragement were issues completely ignored by one party—this time, the teens. Parents, perhaps because their role is often one of support and encouragement, wrote several rules about this.

> Encourage teens in what they do. Praise their achievements and let them know when you do not approve.
> Give teens a strong sense of right and wrong.
> Feelings (both positive and negative) are OK.

DISCIPLINE

What to do when rules are broken? Obviously, some form of discipline is needed—teens as well as parents recognized this necessity. As is clear from the following rules, teens often feel that discipline is mishandled. However, it is also clear that many parents are sensitive and self-questioning about their role as disciplinarians.

From the teens
> Parents should not ground teenagers just for minor things, and when they are grounded, it should be for no more than a week.
> If teenagers do something wrong, don't threaten them; just sit them down and try to figure out why they did it. Explain why it was wrong, and if punishment is needed, then put them on restriction.
> Make punishments relate to what was done wrong.

From the parents
> Teens will not be punished by being confined to quarters and rationing food (can't have any cake, etc.).
> Teenagers should help choose their punishment when rules are broken. Parents need to enforce rules and punishments with consistency.
> Consistently enforced limits indicate care and love.

*　*　*

The rules in this chapter are intended to be fair to everyone living in the household. Some of the rules may seem too lenient, others too strict. The authors of these rules were influenced by the circumstances in which they live and the areas they considered to be problems. After reading these rules, you may have some new ideas about the rules in your household. Ask those with whom you live what they think. Show them this chapter, discuss problems and compromises. It is amazing how the process of discussing how to live together in a manner that is fair to everyone can help the members of a household to understand one another more completely.

5

THREE THINGS I
WOULD CHANGE

ASSIGNMENT:

3 THINGS I WOULD CHANGE
        IN MY LIFE

1. _____
2. _____
3. _____

LIST & WRITE A BRIEF ESSAY—
        DUE MONDAY

JEFF: A SCENARIO

Jeff was tired of it, tired of all the taunts and the names they called him—everything. He had never been one of the athletes; he was too pitifully thin and underconfident to be a jock in the eyes of his peers. He wasn't very popular with the "in" crowd; he didn't have the money or the fashion-sense for that. He wasn't respected by the rebels; he had never really hated his parents. And he didn't fit in with the "A" students; other things were always more important to him than school.

Then, two days ago, everything in his locker disappeared. In its place was a note, part of which read, "Lost all your books, huh wimp? Better run to your mommy, Jeffy." Now he had no books, his self-respect (what little he had left) kept him from telling his mother about it, and, worst of all, someone out there hated his guts. "Why?" he thought, "What did I do wrong?"

Many teenagers are very unhappy about certain aspects of their lives. Some of them blame others for their problems. Others, like Jeff, who feel they don't fit in, turn their frustration upon themselves. But blaming is not a very effective way of dealing with unhappiness. Figuring out what we would like to *change* about a situation often helps us to know what the problem really is, and can be the first step toward a more satisfying life.

This chapter contains excerpts from forty-six essays by students. It deals with parent-teen relationships in the broadest and maybe the best sense: in the sense of understanding one another. The very honest, frequently touching essays quoted here could provide parents with some real insight into teenagers today.

The five areas that students said they most wanted to change are

— their personality

— their physical appearance

— their grades/school performance

— something to do with their parents

— their money situation

Most of the excerpts which follow are arranged under these five general headings. As you read them, imagine a group of students sitting around discussing what they would like to change. You might also imagine a group of adults doing the same thing, and think about how similar or different the discussion would be.

As mentioned in the Introduction, the Parent/Teen Book Group also asked several parents to write about the three things *they* would like to change. Their responses, which were considerably shorter, appear separately at the end of the chapter.

PERSONALITY

>>> I think that if I were more **confident** in myself and my abilities, I would also be more aggressive. Due to this I could get more of what I want to get out of life. If I weren't so unsure of myself and the things I do, I could do more and enjoy my life more fully.

>>> Personality is very important to me. It can make a person likable or make that same person unlikable. My personality is a **very shy** one. I feel uncomfortable around large groups of people. I would like to change this so I could be more outgoing and not have an awkward feeling around people. I think I would have more fun with life and just enjoy it.

>>> I can't accept **rejection** of any kind. This bothers me because sometimes I feel like the whole world is against me. These are the times that I just throw up my hands

and give up. Because of this fault in my personality, I often get into trouble from peer pressure.

>>> If there's one thing I can't stand, it's a **moody** person. Sometimes I just want to kick myself when I get in these moods! I hate when I have bad thoughts about other people, or if I give someone a hard look because they did something dumb, I think, "Why did you do that? They're only human!" Sometimes I find myself **judging people** for one stupid reason, and not giving them a chance! I want to be able to be friendly to everyone, even if they are different from me.

>>> I have many friends that care about me, but when it comes to being totally open towards them, I just can't. I'm worried that they'll think differently about me. Sometimes I'd like to tell them about my problems but I wouldn't want to get them depressed. **I just hide** my problems from them, even though I know they can help.

>>> The first thing I would change would be my feelings towards other people, the **fear of hurting** them or making them feel bad. It's just that my dad told me to never let anyone take advantage or make a fool out of me, but I can't be harmful to anyone. Many people treat me like dirt, but when they need me for anything I try my best to help them in any way I can. It gives me a great deal of satisfaction when I help someone, but it's not all that easy and it's not all that much fun.

>>> I would like to become **more outgoing.** This would help me in my relationships with friends. It would aid me in joining clubs, organizations and sports. I feel this trait would put me in a whole new position, allowing me to enjoy life instead of being jealous of it.

>>> The first thing I would change, would be to make myself be more aggressive. This I would do because I feel that

I am **too passive** and I miss out on quite a few things because I don't reach out for the things that I want.

>>> I would take back all of the bad things I have said to people and **make more of the friends** I could have had.

>>> My temper sometimes gets so outrageous that I can't seem to control it. I would like to be able to **control my temper** in any event. I am too eagerly ready to disagree with something before thinking about it.

>>> **I am lazy,** and changing this problem isn't going to be easy, but I think it will be well worth the effort. My laziness is very clear, especially at school. At home I don't exercise and I don't do my homework. I think that by the end of this or next month I will have improved myself a great deal.

The essay below is typical, discussing personality, looks, and school.

>>> THESE ARE COMMON COMPLAINTS

The three things I would like to change about myself are very simple and common. I would like to change my personality in certain areas, my appearance, and my school habits. I think these are common complaints, but not so easily taken care of.

I have a few major flaws in my personality. First off, I have big problems when it comes to letting people know how I feel. I've always wanted to be able to be straight and forward with people, but I just can't do it. I've been trying to work on that, but it doesn't seem to be working. I also seem to care about things more than other people. This isn't such a big problem, but it's very easy to get frustrated when people don't give a care about the same things you care about. I have this problem mostly with friends. I value friendships higher than a lot of people who don't understand why I think the way I do. I "get off" on talking about people. I get mad at myself when I do things like that, so that's another problem. I let people push me around too. I'm more or less a wimp when it comes to standing up for myself. I cry about things too much and don't do anything else.

Now my appearance is another story. I don't consider myself to be anything else but below normal. I would like to be thinner and pretty, just like anyone else. I've been working on this problem since seventh grade. It will always be a problem to me. I think this is just one of those facts of life you can't change—like eye color for instance. As much as I would like green eyes, I can do absolutely nothing about it!

Then there's always the school work. I have never in my life been a very good student. I have terrible study habits and I don't comprehend a lot of things, like geometry. I would like to bring all my grades up and take tests more seriously. I either forget, or just don't get around to studying. I just want to be smarter.

I live with all this in my life and I'm used to it. As much as I would like to change it, I can't.

Although this essay concludes more pessimistically than many of the other papers, it focuses on issues that are in the minds of most if not all teens. It also raises an issue that seems to be at the bottom of the whole question of change: What *can* be changed, and what is impossible to change, no matter how much we would like to?

PHYSICAL APPEARANCE

>>> I would **change my looks.** I'm not saying I'm ugly now because I'm not. I'm very cute as a matter of fact, with a great body. My looks would be so good that the girls would worship me as I passed by. I'd have the magazine *GQ* calling me every ten minutes so that I would pose for them.

>>> First of all I would want to **change my height.** I would give my eyeteeth to be two inches shorter. I hate being 5'9" with very long legs. Most of my problems with friends and boyfriends would be solved if I were shorter. It is very hard for me to find a guy who is taller or the same height as me. When I do, the guy is only about an inch taller, so if we go out, I can't wear high-heeled shoes, so I don't like to dress up at all! I have never had a friend who has been taller than I am.

>>> To this very day I haven't stopped growing an inch. I'm only fifteen and 6'4". **I don't like the idea of being so tall** because everyone has to look up to me and when I'm at home I can't walk under my ceiling fan without seriously injuring myself. I'm outgrowing my bed every day. I have to ball up into a little ball so that my feet and head don't hang over the bed. Now if I was 5'11", I wouldn't mind at all because I could sleep better and walk in my house without hitting myself on the head.

>>> Now I know for a fact that I don't look like the son of Frankenstein, but **I could look a whole lot better.** I feel I'm too skinny or too bony and that it really doesn't appeal to a lot of women. I wish that I could have kept my weight program going so that I would have broad shoulders and big arms!!

>>> It would be nicer to **change my looks.** I like being blonde, but I wish I were a little taller and really cute. It would be nice if my eyes were deeper blue than they are, too. I don't know if it would make life easier, but it would be fun.

>>> I don't consider myself an extremely prejudiced person, only in the way of social groups. I don't mean to be rude, but all of these people who call themselves "mod" that wear these fluorescent clothes and cut their hair weird really bother me. They aren't all classified as totally weird people, I know some and they are nice, but **it's the outward appearance that bothers me.**

>>> If I were **to change my physical appearance,** I would have started a long time ago. A few years ago I was given a chance to start weight training which I did not do until my tenth-grade year. I would have worked hard and gotten more involved in sports at a younger age. I have been pretty successful in sports. I have to wonder if I could have been a lot better.

Several of the students addressed the possibility of actually making some of the changes they were writing about.

>>> ...AND TO NOT LIE ABOUT THINGS...
Three things I would change in my life would be better grades, especially in high school, a better relationship with my mom, and to not lie about things to get myself out of a situation.

If I could, I would change my grades. When I go to college they will probably say, "I'm sorry Miss Jones, you were not accepted into our college because of your grades." I have not really thought about it that much until now. It is important that everyone gets good grades in high school because it will reflect on you later in life. I didn't put much time in my schoolwork and studying. If I could do it over again I surely would jump at the chance.

Now that I am growing up it is harder for our parents to discipline us. I now know that. I always disliked my mom because she always used to spank me as a child. I thought I had the meanest mom in the world. As a child I seemed to grow away from my mom. As I started to get older I never really knew my mom. All my friends say how they tell their mom everything but I think I'm a little afraid to tell my mom. I would practically do anything to have a good relationship with my mom. Sometimes I feel so alone and lost without her. But we are working on our problem.

Every time I get in trouble for doing something or get caught I lie my way out of it. It started by just one little fib; then it grew to be worse and worse. I feel so guilty after it is blamed on someone else but yet I don't want to get in trouble myself. For example, a couple of weeks ago my mom was looking for something and found that one of her crystal glasses was missing. As usual I denied it because I would be killed. So I blamed it on my brother (who is five years younger than me, eleven years old). After a while I felt so guilty that I confessed to breaking the glass. It's like being addicted to something; it's hard to quit. I know I have to quit because I only hurt myself by lying.

So you have read my story and now you know the three things I would change in my life would be better grades, a better relationship with my mom, and to stop lying. I'm sure there are many more things I would like to change but these are on the top of my list.

SCHOOL AND GRADES

>>> When I first started school, I was scared to death and I wouldn't open up to anyone. I was afraid to try something because I thought, if I failed, I would be laughed at. Then I changed, I discovered my friends, and I turned into Miss Talk-a-Lot! I enjoyed socializing more than academics. If I could start over again, **I would listen more to my teachers and do the best I can** to receive those A's.

>>> I don't get grades that are too bad, but **I would like to do better.** My grades are okay if I want to slide by high school; that's not what I want. I want to make my parents proud of me. I want to come home feeling like I did something right, something for me to be proud of. If I did my work and got better grades my life would be a lot easier.

>>> I would like to change my knowledge. **I would love to master my abilities.** I am a bright person, it is just that I don't know how to use my abilities to my highest potential. Once I learn how to master my study skills I would like to become an A student.

>>> Sometimes I try to be good in school, but there are so many things going on around me that I don't even think about schoolwork. The only time I think about school is when I'm in school. I hope to change in a way that I could come home and **just go straight into homework,** but instead I end up going back out the door.

>>> When I was younger, in about fifth through ninth grade, school was just there. It really wasn't important to me, but I have had to pay for that attitude. My grades were okay but they weren't what colleges are looking for. C's and B's aren't what help make a person successful. It takes A's and B's. **I wish I could change those grades.**

>>> **I wish that I could get A's and B's on my report card.** If I did, it would be a miracle. That would really impress me along with others. It would be really nice if I made it on one of the honor roles. I would not have to feel ashamed of myself for messing up.

>>> **I wish I would have participated in more school activities.** Athletics has always appealed to me, but I never really tried a variety of sports. My life was always too busy and complicated to worry about extra hours after school practicing. Clubs and fund raisers now interest me more than they did the first couple of years of high school. Not being active in school will be regrettable after high school is gone.

PARENTS

>>> **I wish that I could start my life all over again and try harder to get along with my parents.** All the quick, untrue responses directed at them, when fighting, I would think instead of saying. I would try to talk my problems over with them, instead of running and deliberately disobeying them. This attitude has gotten me nowhere and was completely wrong.

>>> **I don't want to be on restriction** because it ruins my social life, being with friends all the time without worries. My parents think that restriction solves everything; they never talk about "what happened" or "why." It's just "You're on restriction!" and that's it. Restriction just keeps me from having fun; it doesn't help me with what I did wrong. I'm not totally against punishment, but I think that restriction doesn't solve a thing.

>>> One of the most important things in my life I feel I would change would be **the way things are going with my dad.** Sometimes he wants us to go stay with him, and both my parents force me to go, even though my mom knows how much it upsets me to go stay with him. I can't really tell my dad that I don't like going to his house, because I don't want to hurt his feelings. However, I become very upset and depressed when I'm told I have to go. It isn't that I don't love my father, and love being with him, it's just that he pushes his religious views on me to such an extent that I feel trapped by my own personal beliefs, and those he feels I should have. Also, when we go to his house, we sit around and do nothing. I don't have to be entertained or doing something all the time, but that's how it goes all weekend. I would change things so we could both somehow benefit from each other's company without having conflicting discussions.

>>> **I would like to change my relationship with my parents.** I'm hardly ever home now that I go to school and have a job. I never sit down with my parents and talk anymore, and it scares me a little.

>>> The most important thing about my life I would change is **the relationship I have with my mom.** We always fight and never get along. I would like to change that by not fighting with her and not getting into any trouble that

she will yell at me for. I don't talk to her that much and I don't help around the house enough. I would change that by working for her more and talking to her more and letting her help me with my problems. My life would be much easier if I got along with my mom.

>>> I think I have a good relationship with my mom. We always do everything together; she's my best friend. But there are things I can't tell her that I can only tell my friends at school. **I wish I wouldn't be so embarrassed to tell her some of my crazy thoughts.** In a sense, she's probably gone through them too.

>>> **I would like to change the fact that my mom and dad are divorced.** That's OK, except that my dad likes to come over to my mom's house trying to get into an argument with either my mom or me. And I am tired of it.

>>> **My stepfather and I hardly can say a few words to each other** without getting into an argument. The major difference between us is my real father. Other differences are my schooling, the guys I like, and how much work I do around the house. We often argue about these things. I know if we could talk, sit down and talk, we wouldn't argue so often. It's just a matter of trying to get along without changing my ways.

>>> **My stepfather is a major issue.** (Or should I say was, because he passed on about two years ago.) Ever since I was two, he treated me, so I thought, terribly. He had a son that was six years older than I. He gave his son everything he wanted. All I got from him was punishment for every little thing I did wrong. My stepbrother, finally being spoiled, got into much trouble. My stepbrother didn't get punishment as harsh as mine. Now that I look back on the situation, I realize that my stepfather did what he did for my own good. He didn't want

me to be like my stepbrother. I now thank my stepfather for what he did. Even though his rules for me were very strict. At the time, I felt very hurt. Now I feel thankful.

>>> **I would change my relationship with my parents, my dad especially.** I would like to be able to ask my parents anything that comes to mind, and talk to them about any problems I have. Of all the things that I could change about my life, I think this one would have to be first.

MONEY

>>> **Saving money** is one thing I wish I would have done. All the dumb knick-knacks I've bought through the years could have bought me a car. To think of all the hours I've spent baby-sitting and cleaning and never saving any money makes me sick. Now I realize the importance of a budget.

>>> I have always had a lot of money to spend, especially to go out with friends. **I wish I could have seen just how much money I had.** It probably would be enough to buy a new car by now or maybe take a trip to Hawaii or Europe. My grandfather said, "Spend half and save half and you will be more happy and secure."

>>> **Money! I would love to have a lot of money.** That way I could buy a beach house, a hot car, and a lot of clothes. I could go to the best restaurants. I could also afford my bills on the house and car. I could go on a cruise to Hawaii. I could fly to Paris and anywhere else in the world.

>>> **I want to have more money** if I could change my life, because it would be easier for me and my family. I would not have had to quit my other high school and I

could be with my friends there. Also my parents would not get in any arguments about money problems.

...AND OTHER THINGS MANY WOULD CHANGE

Getting a Job

>>> I would really like **a good-paying job. Being a teenager, it's sometimes hard to get a job,** and when you find someone to hire you it's usually minimum wage, unless it's a job like picking all the rocks off a two-acre lot. Rotten jobs pay OK. But people either don't trust you or think you can't handle "big" jobs that pay well. I would like to get a chance to earn some big money.

>>> Another thing I would change if I could is getting a job. At the present time it is impossible because I have to watch my little sister after school, but I would like to get **a job that pays reasonably well,** where I can help my mom out financially, while saving a little for myself as well. I'd like to be able to save some money for college, and start on a savings for my Karman Ghia as well, but my mom comes first, and I feel it's really important to help her out.

The Place I Live

>>> One thing I would do is **move near the beach.** If I lived near the beach it would have to be Santa Barbara. I would be able to go surfing or boogie-boarding every day. I could also throw beach parties every weekend.

>>> I've lived in California all my life, and I would love to change that. This doesn't mean that I hate California, it just means I like change. This wish will hopefully come

true very soon when I go to college. I plan to go to another state because I love to **meet new people and see new places.**

Moving Out

>>> The first thing that I would want to change is where I live. It isn't really where I live, but **who I live with.** I don't get along very well with my family and it's hard to live with people I don't get along with. My grandma and grandpa live with us and they have to take care of my two little cousins. They are always screaming and crying and it bothers me because when I don't have to work and I come home after school I want peace and quiet. If I could, I would have a nice little apartment for myself.

>>> I would like to change my home situation because **I am not happy where I live.** I do not get along with my father and my sisters because we constantly disagree on things. My father and I have never really gotten along because he expects too much out of me and he doesn't give me any freedom of choice. He is constantly right and I never get a chance to give my opinion. My sisters on the other hand are always tattling and getting into my things and I never have any privacy.

The Opposite Sex

>>> **I would like to get back together with an ex-boyfriend of mine.** Right now the guy I'm seeing is really nice, I enjoy his company, and I like him a lot, but it's just too hard to get over this other guy whom I've known for almost two years. It's really a strong relationship between us though, because I'm really close to his family. Sometimes I think he feels pressure from them about us. If I could change things between us I'd have had us be as close as we were last year.

>>> One thing I would change is **the way my boyfriend feels about having a close relationship.** I would like him to trust me and himself just a little more. I would like for him not to worry so much about falling in love and getting married. I would just like him to relax and to feel comfortable with what he has. Not to worry about the future, just take life one day at a time.

Finding Time

>>> **I am always rushing and I never have time for myself.** Sometimes even my weekends are taken up. I work four times a week and I have songleading practice three or four days out of the school week. One of my really rushed days would start by getting up at seven o'clock to be in time for school, after school up to practice, and I won't get home till 11:30. After all that then I do my homework. I can't quit school or songleading. I was thinking about quitting work but I need the money. Maybe I'll just work two days a week.

Getting Over the Past

>>> **The time I got arrested was mainly my fault.** All I
wanted to do was to fit into the "crowd." One night, my
friends and I were outside walking around. As we
passed by the corner house, we noticed a bike and a
drum set in the yard. We took the drums and the bike
and put them in my "friend's" garage. After that, we all
went home. My friend, being paranoid, took the stolen
bike and drums to the side of my house. There, he hid
them under the foliage of the bushes. When I woke up
in the morning, a police officer was in the living room
talking to my mother. I was busted.

>>> In my past, like many other teenagers, **I have ex-
perimented with drugs.** By this I mean speed, uppers,
marijuana, and even cocaine once. I used to hang
around with the type of people that nothing mattered to
them except the "party life." I first got into drugs when
my family was having serious problems. One of my
brothers was in a coma because he overdosed, and my
other brother was causing problems in both my real
dad's and my mom's marriages. It seemed, at the time,
that nobody had time for me; there was nobody to turn
to, to talk to. After about a year I totally gave up on
drugs, I found new friends and a new outlook on life.

Living with the Present

>>> **One thing I would want to change about my life would
be my brother.** Not to get rid of him or anything, but just
to try and fix it so that he wouldn't have hemophilia. I
see all the problems he has and it hurts me. He can't
play baseball or football like the other guys his age. He
can't even go out for his high school soccer team because he would not be able to pass the physical. I guess
because we are twins I sometimes hurt when he hurts.

Looking Toward the Future

>>> **I'd like to change my place in this world.** Right now I'm a nobody. No one in New York or Hollywood knows my name. I want to do something successful with my life. I don't want to be someone who blends in with the crowd, I want people to look at me and say, "I wish I could be like her."

>>> **I would be so smart if I could.** I would solve problems for the U.S. president. People would think I was Albert Einstein's son. I would win so many awards. I'd design new buildings, space equipment, and many other fantastic things.

And, finally, here is an unusual response to this essay assignment.

>>> **NO SUFFERING, NO STARVATION, NO MURDER**
It seems changes are always needed in this world. I feel that in order for people to learn and grow, they must use changes to help them. Many changes can be thought of, but I can think of three changes that would help the whole world. They are: no suffering, no starvation, and no murdering.

Suffering is a terrible word because it places a picture of something in your mind—hurting, feeling pain, crying. I would change suffering in the world to more LAUGHING. If all the suffering was turned to laughter, people would, instead of hurting, feel happiness, and the whole world would feel better.

Starvation is something that is going on in too many places, so if I could change starvation I would make a law that says if any person is feeling starvation, he or she will get five billion tons of ice cream, and any other food they want. If this change took place, we would not only get rid of starvation, but we would have a world full of fat, happy little people.

Murder is something that exists and yet a lot of people don't like to talk about it. Murders take away people, and often leave their families in great pain. If I could change murder, I would change it to love. If people would love instead of kill, the world would be a brighter place.

These changes are changes that many people would probably think could never happen, but if one person believes they can make suffering, starvation or murder less common, then that's good enough for me.

THINGS I WOULD CHANGE: PARENTS

A SCENARIO
I'm a thirty-three year old woman with two kids, one fifteen and the other three years old, and I've been happily married for four years to my third husband. The kids and my husband are terrific to each other, but that's not the problem.

You see, I dropped out of high school because of my first pregnancy, and I've never gone to college. Since I don't have a high school diploma, the only job I can get is at a fast food place. At only $3.35 an hour, it's not enough to do anything but pay some bills.

I have never had much free time. I had a job seven months after my first pregnancy, and I was always either getting ready for work, working, or taking care of my baby. Now I'm thirty-three, a wife and a mother, and I've never had a "single life" to myself.

I wish I could change my life.

The Parent/Teen Book Group felt that it was important to find out what adults, parents, would change in their lives, so we asked them—not to write an essay but simply to list three things they would change.

Seventeen parents responded, most of them women, many in "telegraph-ese." The reasons many parents resisted writing this list for the Parent/Teen Book Group are not clear. Perhaps the information was too personal. Perhaps, as we grow older, thinking about "what could have been" or "what could be" becomes too far separated from "what I want," or too painful to share.

The responses we did receive were revealing. Most teen responses had to do with the future, while the adults mostly dealt with the present or looked back to the past, wishing they had done things differently. Here, then, are fourteen parents' responses to the question, "What three things would I change in my life?" presented as each individual gave them.

Parent A:
> I would have gotten a college education.
> I would also have encouraged my husband to go to college.
> I wish we had prepared for the girls' college education better, like investing in property.

Parent B:
> Communication between age groups to eliminate social pressure.
> The truth about sex and drugs and life in general. Peer pressure.
> I would change requirements of college education and special education. Go back to high school and check the records to eliminate useless waste of time.

Parent C:
> I would have changed my education, and stayed in school.
> I would have planned my future better and made more goals.
> The way I grew up. I would have changed that too. I would like to have lived with more money and in a better household.

Parent D:
> More productive use of past and present time.
> Full education early in life.
> Have more patience and understanding.

Parent E:
> I would have lived with my first two husbands for a few months before marriage. It would have prevented the marriage a lot of pain.
> I would have gotten my college education twenty years ago. The older you are, the harder it gets.
> I would have been stricter with my daughters when they were younger.

Parent F:
> I would have waited several more years than I did to marry and have children.
> I would have finished college.
> I would have had only one child or maybe two at the most.

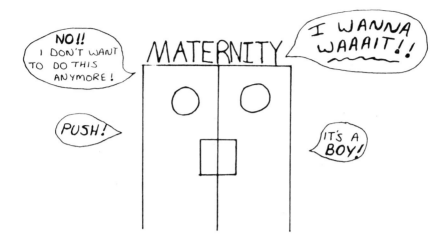

Parent G:
> Would get a better education.
> Would be rich!

Parent H:
> Majored in political science immediately after high school.
> Learned to play the piano.
> Attended a university out of state.

Parent I:
> I would like to be less "busy"—to enjoy simple activities.
> I would like to be able to handle failure in a positive way.
> I would not work when my children are young—until five or six.

Parent J:
> I would, as a responsible, hardworking parent, like someone to take care of *me* once a week. I would like my children to cook and serve dinner once a week (and tuck me in).

Parent K:
> > Move out—peace of mind.
> > Have more time to myself and for myself.
> > Work only halftime.

Parent L:
> > Getting married at seventeen years old.
> > I should have went to college.
> > To have a career, and work, instead of being a housewife.

Parent M:
> > I would take my high school education more seriously.
> > I would wait until I was older before marrying.

Parent N:
> > I would require and monitor more independent reading of literature, since it is not being required in my children's classrooms.
> > I would not have bought the personal TV set for my son's room. Originally it was for video games, but it is too easy to have it aimlessly flicked on.

* * *

What three things would you like to change in your life? If you are a teen or a parent of a teen and one of the things you want to change is your relationships in the family, we hope this book has helped. If not, then we hope that's because those relationships are as good as you want them to be. And whatever your dreams, we hope they take you a long way, are true, and bring you happiness.

AFTERWORD

Few teenagers have had the chance that our group has had, to actually put together a book, learning to do editing, graphics, production, marketing, and promotional work ourselves. It was a long and often hard job, yet every one of us values the experience.

We had many reasons to write this book. First, there was the goal: We were excited about what we had discovered in class, and we wanted to communicate that to others. Then came the process: In turning our class papers into a book, we learned a lot about publishing, more about planning, and even more about cooperation and teamwork. We did a lot of growing.

The Parent/Teen Book Group gained from creating this book. We hope you gained from reading it. We have tried to present a balanced picture, matching most of the teens' comments with those of parents. We wanted both sides to "have their say," and we wanted you, the reader, to have a chance to respond to their statements with a minimum of interpretation on our part. All of us, both teens and parents, are different, and we all see the world differently. Yet we are all constantly raising each other, influencing each other, having our effect on others whether or not we like to admit it. Once we realize that, we can begin to think about the other guy as well as ourselves. We can begin to live in harmony.

We hope that this book says at least that much, and if it makes a difference for just one teen, parent, or family, it will have been worth it.

FROM THE AUTHORS

Cheryl Swain

When Ms. Brondino gave us these essay assignments, I thought they were interesting but I didn't do any of them. I felt guilty about it, so when Ms. Brondino told the class about the book, I thought I'd give it a try. At the first meetings it was kind of uncomfortable because there were a lot of people and we didn't quite understand what we were doing. Then we started going to the publisher's office and working on the computers, inputting the information. Some people had dropped out by then, and we got to know each other a little better. Then things slowed down, and it didn't look like we'd ever get this book finished. Some more people dropped out, and we were left with seven people: five students, Ms. Brondino, and our publisher, Kiran Rana.

Finally things started happening. We were doing more work and getting things done. We all knew what we were supposed to do, and it made it a lot easier to work with each other.

It's been a lot of fun and hard work making this book with my friends. We've all spent a lot of time with each other, and have shared our feelings on things we might not have been able to express otherwise. I'm glad I decided to stick with it. If it weren't for the friends that I made doing this book, I wouldn't have lasted as long as I have. Thanks a lot, guys. I love ya.

Heidi Sonzena

This book has been a learning experience for me, not only because it showed me what working on a book is all about, but also because it taught me to work with different types of people.

Many things came along with the book: working long hours in our publisher's office, trying to force myself to work, and there were also questions of commitment involved.

Yet it has meant a lot to me, and I know what I will say next time someone asks me if I want to write a book!

Scott Coatsworth

I worked on this book for over a year, and it was great. I changed much in that year, and I've come to appreciate many things.

Much of what I learned is about the process of putting together a book. It ain't easy! It takes a lot of teamwork and time. The computer taught me patience; if something goes wrong, it's probably your fault, not the computer's, so you have to stay calm. I also learned how to make contacts and how to keep that calm front for radio and TV. But the most important thing I learned is that people are great. Not all parents are out to get us, and we teens are okay ourselves.

Our Saturday meetings were not always work meetings— often they were therapy, a place for us to work out our problems. We all learned to support each other and to get along, even though we are very different from each other.

The time I've spent on this book has meant the world to me. It is something I know I'll never forget, because it has changed my life in a positive way.

Fran Tulao

The good understanding I have with my family today is a product of being part of the Parent/Teen Book Group. Learning what other parents go through for their children's happiness made me become closer to my own parents.

I dedicate my work on the book and my part in it to my parents, Felicito and Lorceli, and to my grandparents, Juanita and Conception Tulao, and Adriano and Benita Santos.

My feelings about being part of the Group and working on the book are of the utmost gratitude. I felt really good doing what I did; it was a different experience for me. My special thanks to Ms. Brondino for "volunteering" me for the project—I thought I was just waiting for Cheryl so we could go to lunch.

Making a book is hazardous to your social life!

Shellie Brann

My experiences with this book have made me understand a lot about other people and how they feel about certain problems. These parents and teens have been very candid about what's been troubling them. The time that I have spent working with the others in the group has given me a chance to really look at our friendships, and see that it is possible for people from different backgrounds to become good friends. We have all grown stronger in our relationships with each other and with ourselves.

I never really thought that I would ever be friends with anybody in the group besides Heidi. We (Heidi and I) were a lot alike. Then came Cheryl, Fran, and Scott. The five of us have become almost like a family. I've gotten used to all of Scott's little puns, Fran's bubbly and enthusiastic ways of telling us something that normally wouldn't make any of us laugh, and Cheryl always being so quiet when she's with other people and suddenly perking up when it's just us around. All of these people—Heidi, Cheryl, Scott, Fran, and Ms. Brondino—have given me something that I can and will cherish forever: their friendship and their special ways of making me feel like I belong with them. I can never forget that, and I will never forget any of them. I love them all. I hope that once our work is finished we will all stay as good friends as we are now.

Jeanne Brondino

Working on *Raising Each Other* has been a challenging and rewarding experience. I am the teacher in the Parent/Teen Book Group—though a great deal of the time during this project I felt more like a student, I was learning so much. I have been in high school education almost twenty years, and I have taught many wonderful students. Something about this group and our work together will remain very special for me. In the beginning I was inspired by the dedication of everyone in the Group but was unsure about how the book would turn out. By the end I had no doubt that what we had done was good and IMPORTANT.

In my opinion, *Raising Each Other* is a valuable addition to the books available on parent-teen relationships. We have a message, one that is not sensational or trendy. We found that the same basic things work in parenting today as when I was a teenager: trust and honesty, respect and understanding, a willingness to communicate. Even more important: it became very clear to us that, even when it doesn't seem that way, both sides are trying, all the time...

I have two teenaged children; we are trying to raise each other.

LIST OF
CONTRIBUTORS

Students

John Bainer
Dori Baker
Marlene Balber
James Barnes
William Barnes
Michael Bernier
Alvin Boling
William Boykin
Shellie Brann
Tracy Bryant
Eileen Burr
Monica Cardenas
Sergio Carrillo
Natalie Castillo
Stacy Castin
Heather Chamberlain
Scott Coatsworth
Sabrina Cole
Mike Cordeiro
Thomas Crandall
Rebecca Dick
Julia Dodd
Brian Edwards
James Farris
Kris Flower
Kristina Fox
Michelle Fry
Sally Gaucin
Cynthia Greene
Walter Hawthorne

Henry Hayes
Melissa Helzer
Damon Herrell
Xavier Hinojos
Tony Jones
LeAnn Jones
Shannon Luman
Brennon Madding
Michelle Malin
Melinda Matthews
Shelly Meeks
Alex Menkes
Lisa Petersen
Stacey Phillips
Kristina Robledo
Billy Salazar
Angela Schreiner
Heidi Sonzena
Cheryl Swain
Mary Tellez-Giron
Arthur Tovar
Richard Tubiolo
Frances Tulao
Anastasia Vlasic
Christina Vojtko
Deborah Waddell
Lisa Wagner
Nancy Watson
Ginny Wells

Parents

Lourens Klinkenberg	Lucille A. Olson
Brenda J. Swain	Cynthia Delaney
Jack Helm	Mary Moffat
Linda Helm	Nancy M. Patterson
Lana L. Garcia	Laurel Wasserman
Darlene Mason	Verna Leggit
Margie McElroy	Nancy K. Kettle

and others who did not wish to be listed as contributors, plus the 72 anonymous interviews used as the basis for Chapter 2.

Hunter House
BOOKS FOR YOUNG ADULTS

PMS: PREMENSTRUAL SYNDROME
A Guide for Young Women
by Gilda Berger

Premenstrual syndrome can be especially difficult for adolescents. Often it goes undiagnosed, and the resulting behavior may be misunderstood. Proper information is needed, and PMS: A GUIDE FOR YOUNG WOMEN provides this.

Concerned teachers, counselors, and parents can use this book with teenagers to examine the causes and symptoms of PMS. Together, they can explore its suggestions for self-help, including safe diets and relaxation exercises. Other useful sections include the basics of charting, and how to select a doctor.

"By providing reassurance to young women who may think they are alone in their menstrual problems, this book serves as a positive approach to PMS. It discusses ... symptoms, the causes of PMS, visiting a doctor, and self-help suggestions."
—*Current Literature in Family Planning*

Soft Cover ... 96 pages ... $7.95 (New price effective April 1, 1991)

GETTING HIGH IN NATURAL WAYS
An Infobook for Young People of All Ages
by Nancy Levinson and Joanne Rocklin, Ph.D.

"You feel great; you feel like singing at the top of your lungs, and you don't care who is around."

Jogging, dancing, listening to music, or watching funny movies are well-known ways of feeling good. This book also explores the highs that come from *inner* satisfaction. Getting high to many means escaping reality, but these authors show that the highest highs come from being deeply involved in life and the world.

This tremendously positive book can really help young adults develop their inner resources and self-esteem. It is ideal for teenagers who may be experiencing pressure from peers to get high on drugs, and it is an obvious resource for parents, teachers, counselors, and anyone whose life or work is involved with young people.

Soft Cover ... 112 pages ... $7.95 (New price effective April 1, 1991)

Send for our free catalog of books
Family issues, Health and Nutrition, Women's Health, Psychology for Adults and Young Adults. New and Backlist titles.

ORDER FORM

NAME

ADDRESS

CITY/STATE   ZIP

COUNTRY (outside USA)   POSTAL CODE

TITLE	QTY	PRICE	TOTAL
The Enabler		@ $ 6.95	
Exclusively Female		@ $ 5.95	
Getting High in Natural Ways		@ $ 7.95	
Helping Your Child Succeed After Divorce		@ $ 9.95	
Menopause Without Medicine		@ $11.95	
Once A Month *4th Edition*		@ $ 9.95	
PMS: Premenstrual Syndrome		@ $ 7.95	
Raising Each Other		@ $ 8.95	
Trauma in the Lives of Children *(paperback)*		@ $15.95	
Trauma in the Lives of Children *(hard cover)*		@ $24.95	
Writing From Within *2nd Edition*		@ $11.95	

Shipping costs:
*First book: $2.00
($3.00 for Canada)
Each additional book:
$.50 ($1.00 for
Canada)
For UPS or First Class
rates and bulk orders
call us at (714)
624-2277*

TOTAL

Less discount @_____%   (   )

TOTAL COST OF BOOKS   _____

Calif. residents add sales tax   _____

Shipping & handling   _____

TOTAL ENCLOSED   _____
Please pay in U.S. funds only

❏ Check   ❏ Money Order   ❏ Visa   ❏ M/C

Card # _____ Exp date _____

Signature _____

Phone number _____

Complete and mail to:

Hunter House Inc., Publishers

PO Box 847, Claremont, CA 91711

❏ Check here to receive our book catalog